Selina Dolaro

Bella-Demonia

A Dramatic Story

Selina Dolaro

Bella-Demonia
A Dramatic Story

ISBN/EAN: 9783337342562

Printed in Europe, USA, Canada, Australia, Japan

Cover: Foto ©Andreas Hilbeck / pixelio.de

More available books at **www.hansebooks.com**

BELLA-DEMONIA.

A DRAMATIC STORY.

BY

SELINA DOLARO.

We are but pieces in the game He plays
Upon this checker-board of nights and days,
Hither and thither moves, and checks and slays,
And one by one back in the closet lays.

Omar-i-Khayyám.

PHILADELPHIA:

J. B. LIPPINCOTT COMPANY.

DEDICATION.

In Memoriam.

SELINA DOLARO.

Yon rising Moon that looks upon us twain,
How oft hereafter will she wax and wane,
   How oft, hereafter rising, look for us
Through this same Garden, and for *One* in vain!

And when, like her, O Sáki, you shall pass
Among the Guests, star-scattered on the grass,
   And in your joyous errand reach the spot
Where I made *one*,—turn down an empty glass!

OMAR-I-KHAYYÁM.

SHE said to me one day, not long ago, "I wonder whether I shall live to see my book come out, and hear what critics say? I fear I shall not." And her doubt proved just. Madame Dolaro, of whose *self* the world knew but one aspect, that which strove to please its fickle fancy on the mimic stage, has left a world of friends to mourn a loss that few, who knew her not, as some of us, can realize.

Born but a few months more than thirty-five years since, she lived her life with all its disappointments and its joys—neither of which were few—calmly serene in every purpose of her earthly span. When, on the morning of the 25th, we buried what was left to us of her, quietly, as she wished, among the graves of those who died in her ancestral faith, in a green nook among the Cypress Hills, the honored few who, with her to the end, heard her last words and caught her dying breath when on the world she closed her weary eyes, felt that her time had come, and thanked the God in whom through all her pilgrimage on earth she placed her trust with gentle, simple faith, that He had suffered her to end the work she had begun, and, merciful at last, had let her fall asleep in "perfect peace that passeth understanding." For in death, as she had been in life, she lay a sweet ensample to her children and her friends.

She married early—in her fifteenth year—one who, like her, was of the Jewish faith; he traced his ancestry, without a flaw, back to a family who from their home in Spain were thrust in 1492 and sought a safe retreat in Italy. Finding a refuge at Belasco, thence they took their name, discarding that which Spain had known them by,—Miara.

Her artist life began in '70, after some three years spent developing her matchless voice at the Conservatoire of Paris, and she made her first *début* upon the stage that year in "Chilperic" at the Lyceum Theatre. Success crowned every task she 'tempted from the start; the artist world flocked eager to acclaim this prima donna who was but a child, and all the press of England told the world of her rare triumphs in light opera. Later, in "Zampa" and in "Fleur de Lys," in "Madame Angot" and "La Périchole," she showed the public that in opéra-bouffe there may be something more than vulgar jest, suggestive quip, and veiled indecency, throwing around burlesque a zaimph of art. Under the circumstances, 'twas not strange that, presently discarding such light rôles, she trod at last the operatic stage under Carl Rosa's management, and then it was that, conscious of her power, she re-created "Carmen," and at once took, as it were of right, the place reserved for her.

Her "Carmen" first was played in '79,—in February,—and from that time forth it seemed as if her future were secured; but circumstances which proverbially are out of our control ordained that she should cede her place in opera to some one else less fit for it than she had been, and soon we find her once again, with all the cares of management upon her hands, leading her company in opéra-bouffe, only, however, for a while; for next we find her singing "Carmen" in New York,— this time in Italian, and now surrounded by an envious foreign *clique* who strove to hinder her in all she did, till, weary of their petty jealousies, she sought once more her English home for rest. In 1883 she came again, and shone among us here in comedy. She played in "Caste," and those who saw how she won every heart with Polly Eccles' tears have since sought vainly for her like again. Since then until her doul declared itself, she played a vast variety of *rôles*, comedy, burlesque, drama, opéra-bouffe, and charmed us with her tears as with her smiles,—for even in her most Cimmerian hours, Madame Dolaro smiled upon the world that was the better that she lived therein, but used her with such merciless despite, until at last when luck had seemed to turn and some of her desires began to bask in realization, then the strained cord snapped. Her health, which had left much to be desired, gave way without the warning of an hour, and she who yesterday had been the queen of opera and comedy was laid upon a bed of sickness from which those who saw her there ne'er dared to hope that she could rise again, and plucky though she was, she too made up her mind she was to die.

'Twas only in her later years that I was privileged to know her, when the blow had fallen that deprived her of the power to revel in the glorious gift of life; but even then her bravery was such that high above misfortunes such as most men would succumb to, she triumphantly rose, and began her work in life anew: her voice, her strength, much of her sweet self, gone, she turned her hands and brain to other work. Early in '87, when at first her fragile body rallied from the shock of her first seizure, she took up the pen and put the final touches to a play called "Fashion" which she wrote some years ago, but which had never been produced. Hearing the play was ready for the stage, her friends came round her and entreated her to let them act it for her benefit, and A. M. Palmer foremost of them all lent her his stage and its accessories wherewith to mount her brilliant comedy. In May—the 19th of the month—this work received its first production, and was played as perfectly as any drama could, by a well-chosen cast of faithful friends who strove their utmost to make "Dolly's play" a great success. How they succeeded has been written in the annals of the stage. Now she could rest awhile, and by the sea Madame Dolaro and her daughter lived a few short months in perfect peace, and so when she returned to town it almost seemed as if she might be with us soon again as once she had been, but the daily cares, the constant wonder where to turn for work that she could do, began to break again the skein of life that rest had almost weft.

When in the winter-time of '87 her drama "Fashion" was produced and all its beauties marred by rank incompetence of some of those who played it, and "the press" who in the spring had chanted in its praise turned round and said that "Dolly's play" had failed to please the public, then she realized that she must seek more uncongenial work to make her daily bread, and so she wrote articles, stories for the magazines, and made that book entitled "Mes Amours" out of the poems and the doggerel rhymes that she had written and that faithful friends wrote for her, giving her their leave to print their verses. Not content to wait and trust to Fortune for some unexpected gift, she turned at once to the most arduous task of all her life, —"Bella-Demonia." With loving care she labored at her book, reading authorities and histories, and, having gathered her materials, she took them to the sea-shore. There we wrote (hers was the brain and mine the hand alone) "Bella-Demonia: a Dramatic Tale." The world has read how when this book was done and publishers had read it and agreed to publish it the manuscript was lost,—was stolen from the office of *The World* by some malignant fiend whose wickedness the patient lightnings yet have failed to blast. Up to that hour her health had seemed to us improving daily, but this frightful loss seemed such a shock to the poor fragile soul that from that day the end began, and as she bravely sate her down and wrote again her book from memory (for she kept no notes), the hand of Death seemed to be drawing her away from us. The book at length was done over again, and then the Lippincotts made her an offer that she could accept, so that the latter months were lived at least in comfort, if not luxury.

Meanwhile, she made another drama of her book, which still awaits production; it is called "Bella-Demonia," like her novel, and in it she voices the dramatic scenes through which the people of her novel pass. This done, she did not "fold her hands for sleep," but set to work once more and wrote a new novel, which just two days before the end began was finished. She had been down town to see about its publication, when, chancing to call upon her with a friend, we found her lying crimsoned with her life that ebbed from the old deep-hidden wound. That was upon the 19th, Saturday, and from that time with all the care we knew how to bestow we tended her, though we, her children and her friends, knew well that this was the beginning of the coming end.

All Sunday and on Monday just a gleam of hope lit up the twilight of our grief, but Tuesday afternoon the little life began the final struggle to be free. On Wednesday her sharper sufferings ceased, and in the afternoon the look of pain died from her face and one of exquisite contentment took its place. She was so fair! Then, at a quarter after six o'clock, she tried to speak to us just once again, and, gentle, trusting, loving to the last, she ceased to strive to hold her little life, and, weary of her day's work in the world, which for her fragile frame had been so hard, she laid her down to rest and trustingly gave back her soul to God—and fell asleep.

EDWARD HERON-ALLEN.

26th January, 1889.

LIPPINCOTT'S
MONTHLY MAGAZINE.

MARCH, 1889.

BELLA-DEMONIA.

PROLOGUE.

CHAPTER I.

THE HONORABLE JOHN VYVIAN FANE.

"BUT indeed, Excellency, the fare is three roubles."

"Away! and quickly."

"But indeed——"

"What! still whining? Here! take that!"

The sharp shriek of a man in pain rang out in the wintry air, and was lost on the snow-clad Prospect. An *isvoshtshik*—a sleigh-driver—had been struck across the face by the passenger who had just descended from his droschky, at the top of the Newski Prospect.

The *isvoshtshik* was a miserable specimen of the Russian *moujik* or peasant class, clad in the ragged fur coat and pleated boots of his profession, and, as he cowered against the side of his droschky, formed a wonderful contrast to the man who had struck him. The latter stood illumined by the oil lamp that lit the curb hard by (I am talking of the Petersburg of twenty years ago), a figure of military erectness, clad in a long and tightly-fitting coat of dark cloth, heavily trimmed with Astrachan fur; the cap on his head and the gloves on his hands were of the same material, and his feet were encased in high polished leather boots whose simplicity bespoke their English manufacture. The face illuminated as the man turned, by the oil lamp, was finely cut and of an ivory pallor. What was visible of the closely-cut hair beneath the fur cap was of a jet-black, as was also the stiff military moustache which, drawn to fine points on either side, disclosed a thin, pale, cruel mouth. The man looked down at the trembling *moujik*, one hand upon his hip, the other holding a light rattan which still quivered with the force of the blow which had just been laid across the *moujik's* face.

There was nothing very noteworthy—especially at the time of

which I write—in a droschky-driver being struck by his client, but the stillness of the air in the keen frost of the Russian winter seemed to accentuate the bitterness of the cry that rang out. At any rate, it attracted the notice of a man who, stepping from the shadow of a neighboring gate-way, approached the group.

"Come, come," said the new arrival, in the tone of one accustomed to command, "men are not flogged in the streets of Petersburg for nothing. What is the meaning of this?"

The man who had struck the sleigh-driver turned on his heel and confronted his interrogator. The manner of the latter immediately changed, and, straightening his figure as he raised his hand in military salute, he exclaimed, in a tone of surprise,—

"The Gospodar Vyvian Fane! We are punctual!"

As he spoke, the *moujik*, who had fastened his eyes on the new-comer's face, sprang upon the driving-seat of his droschky, exclaiming under his breath as he did so,—

"Dmitri Keratieff, of the Secret Police! Holy St. Katerine, what an escape!" And, before either of the pair could turn, he had started his horse and disappeared down one of the by-streets leading out of the Newski Prospect.

"Yes," said the man whom Keratieff had addressed as Vyvian Fane, in answer to the Police Agent's ejaculation, "my business is of a kind that demands punctuality on my part, promptitude on yours. No need to trouble about this scoundrel—ah! he is gone; it is well. He tried to claim a double fare: he mistook his man."

And the Honorable John Vyvian Fane laughed, a little hard laugh that parted his thin lips over two rows of small cruel teeth.

"You have brought the papers?" queried Keratieff.

"Here they are," replied Fane, drawing a letter-case from his pocket and taking thence a folded sheet. "This one will be more than sufficient. It is a letter from Alexis Dorski, the Terrorist leader, to the Prince Ladislas Galitzin. You will see that it proves the intimacy of the two."

"That will indeed be sufficient," returned the Police Agent; and, hastily unbuttoning the cloak which was wrapped about his somewhat stunted form, the light of a small flat lantern shone out, instantly lit by some chemical process, and illuminating the sheet which Keratieff perused attentively.

"It is more than enough," observed he, as he extinguished the light and refolded the paper, which he, in turn, placed in his pocket-book. "How does the Prince Ladislas come to have let this fall into our hands?"

"He had intrusted it to his sister, the Princess Carita Galitzin, for safe custody. It is from her that it was—obtained."

The Chief of Police glanced quickly and keenly at the impassive face of the Englishman.

"Ah!" he ejaculated. Then, after an instant's pause, he asked, "When do you desire that this arrest should take place?"

"At once. Within an hour he must be safely lodged in the Fortress of St. Peter and St. Paul."

" So soon ?"

" Yes. The young fool was so ill-advised as to attempt to make a scene at the Club to-night. The matter must not be taken up again to-morrow. He must have disappeared. You understand ?"

" Perfectly."

" And mark me, also," continued Fane, lowering his voice, though in the moonlight it was plain that no one was near. " Once in the fortress, he must not come out. There must be no trial."

The Police Agent smiled :

" Have no fear, Gospodar Fane. Prisoners who take the ground-floor apartments of St. Peter and St. Paul seldom come to trial. The place is damp. Life is uncertain. The Prince Ladislas is delicate. By the bye, you might like to assist when—when the time comes. A prison funeral is an interesting thing—to a foreigner."

" Are you sure you can lay your hand upon him at once ?" queried Fane, not appearing to notice the other's words.

" In an hour he will be safely lodged," answered Keratieff, echoing the Englishman's words.

" Where is he now ? He left the Club at once."

" He is with his wife."

" *What !*"

" With his wife. The prince has been more than a year married. A *mésalliance*, Excellency."

" I did not know of this."

" Nor any one else, with the exception of Dmitri Keratieff and the Princess Carita his sister."

" The deuce !"

" There is yet time in half an hour, should you change your mind."

" Change my mind ! Never ! the revenge will be all the finer. What a chance !"

Vyvian Fane was about to leave his companion, when the latter stopped him, laying a hand upon his arm.

" This is a terrible revenge, Gospodar Fane," he said. " It strikes his sister and his wife with him."

" Well ?"

" It will probably kill both these women."

Vyvian Fane had bitten the end from a cigar and had struck a match. As he held the flame close to his face, his dark sinister eyes flashed into those of the Police Agent.

The cruel smile disfigured his face again, as he threw down the match and without a word turned on his heel and strode off into the night.

" What a devil !" said Keratieff to himself, as he looked after the retreating figure. " But all the same an invaluable member of our Third Section." And then, hailing a droschky which had been hovering about as if anticipating a fare, he sprang into it, and disappeared in the direction of the police head-quarters.

As the sound of the sleigh-bells died away in the distance, the moon shone down upon the Newski Prospect and the square of St. Nicholas, which were once more deserted in the frost-bitten air.

CHAPTER II.

HUSBAND AND WIFE.

OF St. Petersburg, as of every other city of the world, the most magnificent and the most squalid dwelling-places abut upon the river. Just as the late Tuileries and the Louvre, in common with the obscurest tenements of the Quartier Latin, look upon the Seine,—just as the Houses of Parliament and Somerset House, in common with the 'long-shore hovels of the city, look upon the Thames,—so in Petersburg the Winter Palace, in common with the warrens of the *moujik* population, looks upon the Neva.

In these warrens live for the most part the students of the city; here it is that the majority of Nihilist intrigues foster and spread, and here it is that the domestic spy, the *dvornik*, or *concierge*, is most looked after and best paid by the Secret Police. It is here also that tenements can be found whose *dvorniks* are better paid by the tenants than by the police, and where individuals who desire to efface themselves conceal their identities behind passports either fictitious in themselves or issued to worthy citizens who have died or disappeared long ago.

In a blind alley leading from the inner court of one of the most intricate blocks of buildings we find with difficulty a low door, an-nouncing a squalid interior, to all appearance a stable or warehouse. We might knock here for an hour without evoking any sign of human habitation, but draw a stick or stone lightly across the door and we are answered by a single word whispered inside. A couple of these passwords are exchanged, and the door opens noiselessly.

Immediately the foot-fall is muffled by the furs with which the hall-way is strewn. We pass through heavy curtains and reach the innermost room of this abode, which, lit entirely by sky-lights and softly-burning lamps, is a very jewel-box. The apartment into which we have penetrated is carpeted with Ukraine and Siberian skins, the walls are hung with silks from Ispahan and embroideries from Damas-cus. The furniture is of the carved ebony from the banks of the Indus, ancient weapons of Turkish origin are festooned upon the silken walls, and on the tables are scattered the gold and silver trinkets of Indian and Persian master-workmen. An inlaid lute of Venetian craft lies upon a chair, an Angora cat is stretched asleep upon another, at opposite ends of the room hang masterpieces of Flemish and French art, in a corner stands a marble statuette from some Florentine *atelier:* in a word, all that luxury and taste can conceive is grouped here as a proper setting for the woman who lies upon a huge divan, nestling among the piled-up cushions in her garments of soft clinging silks,—waiting.

The woman who waits is the Princess Nadine Galitzin, once the handmaiden of the Princess Carita, and now the wife of the young Prince Ladislas.

Yes, the Prince Ladislas Galitzin had made what the world would have stigmatized as a *mésalliance*, but no one would doubt for a mo-ment, looking at the woman as she lies on her divan, that some strain of noble blood, a bar sinister if you will, made her worthy to share the title even of the last Prince Galitzin.

As she lies waiting the advent of her husband, her mind wanders back over all the ecstasy of the past two years. She lives over again the happy days in the château by Ladoga, where she lived more the companion and sister of the Princess Carita than her handmaid,—the arrival from college of Prince Ladislas,—the gradual awaking in her soul of the conviction that this was the Kamar-al-Zaman of her dreams, the King of the Time for her. She remembers the steps in their courtship, the first time that their eyes met and rested in each other, and the death thenceforth of the indifference of the maiden to her mistress's brother; their sudden meeting in one of the corridors, when the prince had clasped her in his arms and kissed her for the first time and then fled without a word; then the progress of their secret betrothal, so sedulously concealed from the old Prince Galitzin; the misery with which she learned of his approaching departure to take up his commission in the Tzar's body-guard, the Regiment of the Transfiguration, and how the prince persuaded his old tutor the family chaplain to marry them secretly in the chapel of the château; their flight to Petersburg; the joys of the year that had elapsed since then,—the greatest of all, perhaps, the day when the Princess Carita had come to her hiding-place to welcome her by the sweet name of sister.

The concealment of their marriage had been a matter of vital necessity. The young Prince Galitzin, last of his branch of a family exalted throughout the history of the Empire, had in his wild student days been suspected of liberal views, and the Tzar had designed for him a brilliant marriage with the daughter of one of the oldest conservative families of his realm. Hence his position in the body-guard; hence the necessity for the concealment of his marriage. Only one besides his sister knew of it, and that was Dmitri Keratieff, Chief of that Third Section,—the secret police that, even to-day, make life in Russia a perpetual terror. But Dmitri Keratieff owed much to the Galitzin family, and with him the secret was safe until such time as its keeping should conflict with his devotion to his master.

The Princess Nadine lay anxiously awaiting her husband : her state was delicately precarious, and the mystery that surrounded her sometimes told hard upon her. Suppose anything should happen? The secret police, she knew too well, acted blindly like the Council of Ten upon denunciations made by unknown enemies. If such a fate should befall her idol, what would be his doom,—and hers? At the thought, recurring as it did to-night with tenfold persistence, she buried her head in the cushions and groaned rather than cried,—

"Husband! husband!"

A rattle of the rings of the hangings, a strong step upon the piled-up furs, and he is with her.

"Nadia—*matiouchka* [little mother], beloved! I am here!"

She is in his arms in an instant; all her misery, all her apprehension, is lost in the ecstasy of his kiss. Yes, he is safe,—safe from all harm; for no one can disturb them here. Their secret is too well guarded. She has no fear.

"I have been so frightened, Ladislas: every hour that you are not with me I torture myself with fears for you. Suppose they should discover me? Perhaps they would look upon your disobedience to the Tzar as cause for your arrest,—for—for anything. Oh, be careful, beloved; should anything befall you it would kill me,—would kill us both. Think of that other life that shall be so dear to us, Ladislas."

"Courage,—courage, Nadia!" he replies. "There is no danger. We cannot be discovered, sweetheart. I know how lonely, how dull you must be. Well, to-night I have a surprise for you: we expect a visitor."

"A visitor?" A look of alarm creeps into the beautiful eyes as she echoes his words.

"Yes. You have heard me speak of Alexis Alexandrovitch?"

"Alexis Dorski, the Nihilist!"

"The same. My old college companion, unknown even to the faction of which he is the leader, comes to Petersburg to-night. I want him to see my wife, my pride. He is coming here."

"Oh, Ladislas, how imprudent you are!"

"Not at all. I have the fullest knowledge that his presence here is unsuspected. Nothing can ever assail Alexis Dorski if he so wills it. Have no fear, darling."

As he speaks, the old servant who alone waits upon the Princess Ladislas Galitzin enters the room.

"What is it?"

"A peddler, an old man armed with the passwords and countersign, desires to speak with your Excellency."

"Admit him."

The servitor retires, and a moment later, lifting the hangings, gives entrance to a bent figure carrying a pack. As soon as the servant has left them the peddler rises to his full height. With a gesture he flings off his disguise of hair and beard and stands before them a young giant.

"Alexis Alexandrovitch!"

"Ladislas Ladislaievitch!"

And the two men are locked in each other's arms.

CHAPTER III.

THE ARREST.

"At last, after so many years, old friend!" It is the Prince Ladislas who speaks, holding the other by the hand. Then, turning to the woman whose frightened eyes are fixed upon the new-comer, he says, "Nadia, this is my old friend Alexis Alexandrovitch Dorski."

"I have heard much of you from my husband, Alexis Alexandrovitch," said she, raising her eyes once more to Dorski's, and addressing him in the familiar Russian fashion. "Welcome to our hiding-place and our home."

"No doubt you fear me, princess," returned Dorski; "but your fears are groundless, believe me. No word or act of mine can implicate your husband. I sought this interview to tell you so."

" I pray that it be so," said the Princess Nadine.

" Well, and how goes the cause?" put in Ladislas Galitzin, cheerily.

" Bravely," replied the other, "both here and in the provinces. We have friends at court, high up,—very high,—in the Regiment of the Transfiguration, as in all three sections of the police. A few years, maybe, a few months, perhaps, and Russia shall be free. What Alexander the Second has done for us already he will do again. He will add to his reforms, and Russia will be free. If not——" And his sentence closed with significant silence.

The princess turned a look of fear towards her husband.

" Have no fear, *matiouchka*," replied the latter, interpreting her look. " I am no conspirator. Alexis and I are friends, but no more. I am not one of his lieutenants. By St. Katerine !" continued he, with a laugh, " I care too little for it all to risk my neck. I am too much at peace with the world, too happy with you, sweetheart, to bear ill-will towards any man, be he Tzar or *moujik*. No, I was never made for a Terrorist. I left that all behind me when I left college; and when our secret society that was to do such wonders was broken up without my being implicated, why, I thought myself well out of it, and settled down as a respectable married man." And he laughed again carelessly as he threw himself on the divan beside his wife.

" Right !" exclaimed Dorski. " That is as it should be. Do not let us say anything more about it. See, I have brought you something." So saying, he drew from his pocket a little leather case. Opening it, he disclosed a portrait of himself set round with opals, which he handed to the princess.

" It is a little wedding-present, though it comes late for the wedding," said he. " But it may serve to impress upon your mind the features of a man who would willingly give up his liberty, and, if needs be, his life, for your husband."

" I thank you, Alexis Alexandrovitch," replied the woman. " I shall cherish your present. But why did you let them set opals round it? I think they will bring us misfortune. Am I not foolish?"

" Yes, indeed," cried Ladislas, " by all the saints, a most excellent portrait, old friend. It shall be one of our greatest treasures."

The three stood together looking at the miniature, when suddenly the stillness was broken by three heavy blows upon the outer door, and by a voice crying, in the silence of the night,—

" Open, in the name of His Majesty the Tzar !"

Every face became white as they exchanged glances; Ladislas hurriedly thrust the portrait into his pocket, and Dorski exclaimed,—

" Great heaven! I am discovered! And yet,—it is impossible. My presence is undreamt of. No matter; hide me,—somewhere,—anywhere."

" Here,—here,—quick," whispered Prince Ladislas, pressing a spring in the frame of one of the large pictures. The picture swung out from the wall, disclosing an open space behind it, contrived in the building. " In here; and do not utter a sound."

"Do not betray my presence by word or look," whispered Dorski, gathering up his pack and his disguise, and stepping into the recess. "I will not be taken alive."

Ladislas Galitzin hurriedly closed the picture, and took his place on the divan beside his wife, who was more dead than alive with terror. Meanwhile, the blows on the outer door and the summons were repeated.

"Open, in the name of His Majesty the Tzar!"

"Open the door!" cried Prince Galitzin, loud enough to be heard outside. "There is no reason why the inmates of this house should fear the mandates of our father the Tzar."

Footsteps sounded in the corridor, a clank as of arms was heard, and Dmitri Keratieff stepped into the room.

"What is the meaning of this?" demanded the prince, haughtily. "See, you have terrified my—my—mistress almost to death. We harbor no suspected persons here."

"My business is with you, Excellency."

"Indeed! Name it."

"I hold a warrant for your arrest on a charge of treason against the sacred person of His Majesty."

"Of treason!—I? Monstrous! Of what am I accused?"

"Of complicity with the traitor Alexis Dorski."

"He is not here! he is not here!" cried the princess, recovering consciousness in time to hear the police-officer's last words.

"I know it," replied the latter. "The police is well informed of his movements; he is now in the Ukraine. The prince is arrested, however, on the evidence of a letter he has received from Dorski, and which is in the hands of the police."

"His letter!" exclaimed the prince. "How——"

"Enough said," broke in the officer. "We cannot enter into explanations. Your Excellency will follow me?"

"Yes." Ladislas was about to follow him, when suddenly the portrait of Dorski flashed across his mind. Quick as thought his hand sought his pocket where it lay; but the keen eye of the Chief of Police caught the action, and, supposing the prince to be in search of some weapon, he sprang upon him, crying out as he did so a word of command in Russian. Two soldiers entered the room. At a sign from Keratieff they seized the prince's arms. Then Keratieff, putting his hand into the prince's pocket, drew forth——the miniature!

"Ah!" he exclaimed, "there needed but this. A portrait of the traitor himself carried on the prince's person. Come. Let us go."

"Send out your soldiers for a moment, Keratieff," said the prince. "I have something to say."

Keratieff gave the word, and the soldiers retired.

"Where am I to be taken?" asked Prince Galitzin.

"To the Schlusselburg."

At the word the prince turned paler yet. Then, commanding himself, he said,—

"Keratieff, you and I know too well what this means. This lady is my wife: let me be alone with her for five minutes. You will not refuse me. I give you my word that I will await you here."

"So be it," returned the Chief of Police, softened in spite of himself as he took in the condition of affairs at a glance. "In five minutes I will return." And he left the husband and wife alone.

As soon as he was gone, Ladislas Galitzin flung himself by the side of his wife, and whispered eagerly in her ear:

"Nadia,—*matiouchka*,—look up, beloved. All may yet be well. They have no suspicion that *he* is here. When I am gone, aid him to escape. Tell him that this is Vyvian Fane's work: I insulted him in the Club to-night. If anything should befall me, bid him avenge me, and you. My poor darling, how can I leave you thus, now? Send at once for Carita. She will care for you till I am free,—and longer, if need shall be. Come, come, be brave. See! I am not afraid!"

And so in agony he tried to soothe, to comfort the paralyzed woman. It seemed like an instant only when Keratieff appeared, pale and silent, at the door.

They went out together.

In the outer street a droschky awaited them, into which Keratieff stepped with his prisoner. The two soldiers followed on horseback as the party moved off in the night.

An hour later the same droschky drove away from the ferry landing of the Fortress of the Schlusselburg. As he made for his hovel by the Neva, the *isvoshtshik* said to himself,—

"So that was your business with the Gospodar Keratieff, son of a dog! Ah! scoundrel, ah! filth, you would strike me with your cane, would you? We shall see; we shall see. The Terror is sometimes as powerful as the Secret Police!"

CHAPTER IV.

A NIHILIST LEADER.

MEANWHILE, as he heard the sound of the sleigh-bells vanish in the distance, Alexis Dorski, opening the picture-frame from the inside, stepped into the room in which the arrest had been made.

The Princess Galitzin was lying motionless upon the divan. Kneeling by her side, the Terrorist endeavored to rouse her.

"Princess," he whispered, "rouse yourself, I implore you. The night grows old, and I must away. Rouse yourself, and listen to me."

Raising herself as if with great difficulty, the eyes of the princess met those of the Nihilist. As they met, she shrank back with a start, exclaiming,—

"Leave me! leave me! I cannot bear to look at you! It was for you they took him."

"Nay, Nadine Fedorovna, it was not for me. Some private revenge has been at work to-night, and—hear me—I swear by the Holy Saints and my devotion to the cause of Liberty that I will avenge your husband. Tell me, has he never mentioned any enemy by name?"

"Yes, yes: he bade me tell you! It has been the work of the Englishman, Vyvian Fane. Swear—swear to me that if they kill Ladislas you will avenge him!"

"I swear it. If this charge is proven against this Vyvian Fane, should it be the work of my whole lifetime, I will punish him. I have sworn it!"

"Thank you,—thank you, Alexis Alexandrovitch! Ah! but what agony!" And with a convulsive movement the woman buried her head in the cushions once more.

Alexis Dorski stood looking down at her. In an instant his keen instinct had taken in the gravity of her condition: he realized that if a triple murder were not to be the work of the night's arrest, aid must be summoned immediately. Bending over her prostrate form, he whispered, in a tone whose softness would have made his desperate followers marvel,—

"Tell me, Nadine Fedorovna, have you no friend that I can call, —no woman——?"

"Carita! Carita!" she moaned, between her clinched teeth.

Rising and hastily resuming his disguise, Dorski went out into the night.

* * * * * * * *

Half an hour later the *dvornik* of the Galitzin Palace was roused by a knocking on his door.

"Dog of a reveller, what wantest thou at such a time?"

And there came back through the door the almost whispered words,—

"In the name of His Majesty and of the Third Section, a message for her Excellency the Princess Carita Alexandrovna."

Hastily tumbling out of his improvised bed, the *dvornik* opened the door. There stood on the threshold an old peddler.

"Deliver this to one of the princess's women at once. It must reach her hand immediately. You understand?"

"Yes, Excellency," replied the *dvornik*, accustomed to seeing the emissaries of the secret police in every form of disguise.

And half an hour later the *troïka* of the Princess Galitzin swept out from under the gate-way and disappeared in the direction of the Neva.

It still wanted three hours of daylight, and the peddler, having delivered his summons at the Galitzin Palace, thought for an instant, and then stepped off at a brisk pace down the broad Prospect, towards the square of St. Katerine, where three or four droschkies stood, awaiting the chance of a night-customer.

As he passed the group of *isvoshtshiks* that stood smoking in a door-way he laid one hand upon his hip, the fingers pointing earthward, raising the other to his ear. As he did so he ejaculated the familiar greeting,—

"*Zdrastvouïtaï*" ("Good-night").

And one of the group answered with a guttural "*Choroshho!*" ("All right!")

The peddler pursued his way.

The *moujik* who had answered his salutation, after a moment's delay, bade his companions good-night, and, mounting the driving-seat of his droschky, started off in pursuit of the peddler. He passed him under a lamp, and as the peddler repeated the motion he had previously made, the *moujik* drew his horse towards the curb, and held out a hand palm upward, as if ascertaining whether it rained or not.

"The night is fine," said the peddler.

"The air is free," said the *isvoshtshik.*

"The air is Russian," said the peddler.

"Men must have air," said the *isvoshtshik.*

"*Choroskho !*"

The droschky drew up, and without a word the peddler got in and was driven a few yards down a by-street. Here he said, "Halt!" and the droschky stopped. The peddler alighted, and, drawing a small object from beneath his arm, held it up to the *moujik.* It was a small gold disk on which was enamelled a red cross.

"Holy St. Nicholas!" ejaculated the *moujik:* "it is the Chief. What are my lord's commands?"

"One of the *isvoshtshiks* of Petersburg drove a prisoner from the Neva to one of the fortresses to-night. You will bring him to this address at ten o'clock in the morning." And the peddler wrote a few words on a slip of paper, which the *isvoshtshik* read carefully and then destroyed.

"If he be alive, he will be there, Excellency."

"Good! Salutation and freedom !"

"Amen. Salutation and freedom !"

And the pair parted once more in opposite directions.

At the time appointed next morning, Alexis Dorski sat before the stove in a room of one of the houses of a quiet suburb of St. Petersburg. He was immersed in thought, but looked up expectantly as the clock struck. He had not long to wait. Almost immediately the *moujik* whom he had accosted on the Newski Prospect entered, accompanied by the one whom we met at the opening of this history.

After casting over him a keen glance of inspection, Dorski and the new-comer exchanged three or four almost imperceptible signs and countersigns. He was apparently satisfied with his examination, and said,—

"Last night you were employed by the police."

"Yes, Excellency."

"To what ferry did you take the prisoner?"

"To the ferry of the Schlusselburg, Excellency."

"Good God! Know you anything of the arrest?"

"Yes, indeed, Excellency," answered the *moujik,* eagerly, "that do I. Earlier in the evening a foreigner hired me to take him to the head of the Newski Prospect. There, when I demanded my fare, he struck me with his cane: see, here is the scar: it will be weeks healing. There he was met by the Gospodar Keratieff of the police, and, burning with fury, I hung about. When they parted, Dmitri Keratieff took me to police head-quarters, thence to the Neva, and thence with his prisoner to the Schlusselburg Ferry. Ah! dog of a foreigner! wait for me !"

"Did Keratieff address the foreigner by name?"

"Yes, Excellency: it was—it was—Ivan—something."

"Vyvian Fane?"

"Yes! yes! that was it, God be praised! I could not remember."

"Good! That will do. Your name?"

"Rodia Pouschkoff."

"It is well. Good-day. Salutation and freedom!"

"Amen. Salutation and freedom!"

The two *moujiks* left the room.

"Now, Vyvian Fane,—since that seems to be your name,—the issue remains between you and me. If the fate of the Schlusselburg befalls Ladislas Ladislaievitch, beware! The world is not wide enough to hide you from the talons of the Terror!"

CHAPTER V.

THE PRINCESS CARITA.

Two days have elapsed since the events occurred which are recorded in the preceding chapter.

In one of the lower rooms of the Galitzin Palace, fitted up as a boudoir, the Princess Carita Galitzin sat at her writing-table, her head resting on her hands. She was dressed in black, and her sable garments served to heighten the pallor of her face no less than the red eyelids that announced the fact that she had been weeping.

Every few minutes she would eagerly look through the papers on the desk before her, as if in search of something which she sought in vain.

At last she is roused by a footstep in the corridor. The hangings of the door part and fall together again, and the Honorable John Vyvian Fane enters the room unannounced.

"Well," he says, by way of greeting, as he flings himself into a chair, "at last Madame la Princesse is good enough to send for her devoted slave, after an absence from home of forty-eight hours. Pray, what new intrigue, what new *amourette*, is engrossing the Princess Carita's attention?" The cruel sneer is on his lips, a tone of raillery is in his voice.

"I have been at the death-bed of two of your victims," she replies, never taking her eyes from his.

"You speak in riddles, princess."

"No, I speak plainly. You have killed a woman and her child by way of revenging yourself upon a man who never harmed you, whose only crime was to know your true vile self."

"What do you mean?"

"I mean that you have caused the arrest of my brother by means of a letter that he confided to me for safe-keeping, and which you, cowardly thief that you are, have stolen from this bureau."

"I am sorry, of course, to hear of your brother's misfortune, but a man who is in communication with traitors to the Tzar has no business to get married,—especially clandestinely."

The princess rose and came close to him.

"How did you know," said she, "that I was speaking of my brother's wife?"

The man saw his false step immediately, and endeavored to retrieve it.

"I did not know," he stammered : "I only assumed. You seemed so excited that I concluded——"

"Cease lying to me, John Vyvian Fane! I do not expect you to show mercy, but I look at least for shame, even from you. What have you done with the document you have stolen?"

"Really, princess, this scene is beginning to pass the possibilities. If your brother has been arrested for treason, I am of course sorry, for it must naturally entail unpleasant consequences upon you. If he has been so foolish as to make a secret marriage, I am of course sorry for his wife. If, as you say, she is dead, I think she is better off than she would be as the wife of a convict with a ' wolf's passport' to Siberia. This is all I have to say."

"You hound!"

"Take care, princess. I am not accustomed to insult of this kind, and I will not allow it even from you. Do you hear me? I will not allow it! Do you think that I am a man to be played with? I think I have given you proof ere now to the contrary. Be good enough to remember what I say!"

For all reply the princess pointed to the door.

"Go!" said she, "and never let me see your coward face again. Go, I say, or I will summon my servants and have you thrown out,—ay! thrown out,—and I will take the consequences of my action. Do you think I, Carita Galitzin, fear you, police spy though you have proved yourself to be? You hear me. I am ready to take the consequences, I tell you."

"In any case," returned Fane, with a violent effort at self-control, "I see that it is useless to prolong *this* interview. I leave you now; but I will return when you are prepared to listen to reason. I deny all your charges against me, and at some future time I will prove to you that any trouble your—relations may be in they have brought upon themselves. Good-morning. Mind! when I return you will be civil : at present I can make excuses for you."

And, with a feeble attempt at nonchalance, the Honorable John Vyvian Fane left the room.

Left by herself, the Princess Galitzin buried her head once more in her hands and resumed her interrupted chain of thought. At last she rose, and, hastily effecting some changes in her toilet, she prepared to leave the house. Whatever was to be her brother's fate, she must seek an interview with him at once; and well she knew the difficulties that lay before her in encompassing her end.

All that day she flew from official to official, from minister to minister; she even sought and obtained an interview with the Tzarewitch himself, and nightfall saw her, provided with the necessary passes, at the ferry of the Schlusselburg, accompanied by a captain of the military police.

CHAPTER VI.

IN THE FORTRESS OF THE SCHLUSSELBURG.

ON one of the islands that cluster in the mouth of the river Neva rises a gaunt pile of buildings, within hailing-distance of which no boat save one ever approaches. It is the dreaded Fortress of the Schlusselburg, one of the great prisons where political suspects are incarcerated. The other is the Fortress of St. Peter and St. Paul. The Schlusselburg has been dramatically described by an American writer as follows: " The guards are so thick on the banks of the island that they can speak to one another, and their orders are, as they pace their beats, to shoot any person who attempts to land. No warning is given, no password is asked. As soon as the foot of a stranger touches the turf on the banks of the island a bullet is fired at his heart. His body falls into the stream and floats down to the sea. No questions are asked. Only one boat is allowed to land on the island; that is painted black and belongs to the police. No one has ever returned from that prison. People may have been released from it, but if so they have never confessed the fact; and the popular belief is that whoever lands there once never leaves alive except to go to Siberia."

It was hither that the young Prince Ladislas had been brought, and at nightfall on the day of which we speak the Princess Galitzin took her seat in the boat to gain the fortress on a visit—an unheard-of concession—in company with the two officers.

She was met at the entrance to the fortress by the chaplain of the prison, an old parish priest, a *batiushka* who had found his way thither twenty years before for having sympathized with and ministered to some dying Nihilist.

The old man's face was inexpressibly sad as he greeted the princess with the benediction of the Church.

" We must be brave, my daughter," he said. " The prince your brother is grievously ill. On the night of his arrival he was confined in one of the lower cells, and the cold and damp attacked him. You must be prepared for a great change."

" My God! is he dead?"

" No, my child."

" He is dying?"

" We are in the hands of God!"

She laid her hand upon his sleeve:

"Tell me, *batiushka*. They have poisoned him?"

The priest made the sign of the cross as he replied once more,—

" We are in the hands of God, my daughter. Come with me. They have moved him into one of the upper rooms."

*   *   *   *   *   *   *   *

In a room looking out over the city, whose lights twinkled across the water, the Prince Ladislas lay dying. That was obvious to the princess the moment she laid her eyes upon the wasted form and drawn features. The film of death was growing over his eyes. For a moment he hardly seemed to notice her; then, raising himself with an effort for an instant, only to fall back upon his pallet exhausted, he whispered,—

"Carita—you! Nadia,—where is she?"

"Ladislas,—brother,—my God! how can I tell you!" And she sank on her knees by the dying man's side.

He raised himself again on one elbow.

"Where is she? Why do you not answer? Holy Mother! has he killed her, too? Yes! yes! She is dead,—my wife, Nadia; is it not so?"

He was answered only by the broken sobs of the prostrate woman.

"Carita," he whispered, with fast-failing breath, "you will avenge us, you and Alexis. Listen: it was the Englishman Vyvian Fane that betrayed me. He stole the letter from you: how he did it I cannot tell; it matters not. Keratieff has it. You swear this?"

"I swear it, brother!"

"Thank God! Come closer. I cannot see you, but you are there, are you not, *matiouchka* beloved——"

A deep sigh ended his sentence, which his sister caught in a last wild kiss.

The Prince Ladislas was dead.

She had arrived but just in time.

The clocks were striking midnight as the princess landed once more at the ferry pier.

Her *troïka* awaited her, and she was swallowed up by the night.

CHAPTER VII.

A WOMAN'S VENGEANCE.

EARLY in the day that succeeded the death of the Prince Ladislas Galitzin in the Fortress of the Schusselburg, the Chief of the Secret Police, Dmitri Keratieff, sat in his office, pondering over the events of the last few days. The Chief was not satisfied with the turn that affairs had taken. In the exercise of his duties as commander of the dreaded Third Section many a cruel task had fallen to his lot to perform; often he had known himself to be the instrument of private vengeances which he had had to work out or be himself suspected of sympathy with the omnipresent agents of the Nihilists. But this time he felt that he had been the compulsory party to a crime that surpassed any in his official experience in cold ferocity. It was therefore with a new feeling of distaste and apprehension that he read on the card that had been brought him by one of his subordinates the name of the Princess Galitzin.

Still, there was no reason that he could allege for not receiving her, whilst there existed, as he knew, many why he should do so, and finally he gave orders that she should be admitted.

She entered the room a moment later, and seated herself opposite to him. Thus placed, they regarded each other in silence for the space of a full minute. At last the Police Agent spoke:

"What can I do for you, madame?" said he.

"You can do me the first and last favor that any member of our family will ever ask of you in return for all or any that we have done for you, Dmitri Semenovitch."

The Chief of Police fidgeted uneasily in his chair. He did not like the proem; but all he said was,—

"Pray proceed. Anything that I can reasonably do for the Princess Galitzin shall be done."

"Good!" replied she. "This is what I require. My brother, as you know, is dead. His arrest was the death-blow of his wife, of whose existence you alone besides myself were aware. She died in my arms, and her child with her, the night after Ladislas was taken from her. I demand from you the documents on which he was arrested."

"Princess," replied Keratieff, "in the first place I do not admit the existence of any document that led to the late Prince Galitzin's arrest; but, even if such were the case, what you ask would be impossible. Supposing that such documents existed, I should be responsible for their safe custody, and were they to leave my hands I should get in exchange for them 'a wolf's passport,' as they say. And the Siberian mines at my time of life are not a thing to be played with."

"One moment," returned the Princess, "and I will prove to you that I am already well informed. The Prince Ladislas Galitzin was arrested in consequence of a letter written to him by the Nihilist leader Dorski. This letter was stolen from *me* and delivered to you by one of your foreign agents, the *Honorable* John Vyvian Fane. By all the rights of common gratitude I demand this letter of you, as a man."

"Princess," replied Keratieff, imperturbably, "I am not in a position to admit the correctness of your—surmises. I do not know, as a man,—the capacity in which you make this request of me,—that Mr. Vyvian Fane has any connection with this department. If you have nothing more to urge, I must beg you to conclude this interview, which, believe me, is as painful to me as it is to you."

For a few moments the princess remained in silent thought. Then, as if with an effort, she made up her mind, and, turning once more to Keratieff, who had risen as if to terminate the conversation, she said,—

"Dmitri Semenovitch, I will say no more of the relations which have existed between our respective families. I appeal to you as a man no longer. But as head of the Russian police you have been made perforce the repository of many family secrets, many details of domestic dramas reach your ears. I am going to recount to you the incidents of a tragedy more bitter than any you yet have heard within these walls. Listen!"

*   *   *   *   *   *   *   *

An hour later, at the close of her story the Chief of Police rose from his seat, and, going to an iron chest that stood in the corner of the room, he took thence a paper, which he handed to the princess.

"What you have told me," said he, gravely, "convinces me of your right to this document. Here is the letter stolen from you by John Vyvian Fane: he confessed the theft to me when he delivered it to me as the *pièce d'accusation* on which the arrest took place. Make your mind easy, madame. This Englishman will leave the country at once, never to return. In three days from now he will cross the frontier."

"At last! at last!" thought the princess, as she was rapidly borne through the streets of Petersburg, ten minutes afterwards. "I have my proofs, and you shall be avenged, Ladislas, and you, Nadia, sweet sister mine. My God, I thank thee!—I thank thee!"

Five days later St. Petersburg rang with the news that the travelling-carriage of the Honorable John Vyvian Fane, whose figure had been a prominent one in the festivities of the past season, had been attacked by brigands just over the Polish frontier, and that the Englishman had been massacred.

That night the Princess Galitzin fell on her knees in the oratory of the Galitzin Palace and cried aloud to God,—

"Vengeance is mine! vengeance is mine!"

And the chaplain, entering the oratory a moment after, found her in floods of tears, the first that she had shed since the murder of her brother.

BOOK I.—VIENNA.

CHAPTER I.

A MASQUERADE BALL.

THE grand masquerade at the Vienna Opera-House, of the 15th August, 1876, was at its height.

Round about the corridors, in and out of the boxes, over the floor, the stage, and the balconies, surged the bedlamite crowd of foolishly-dressed men and dominoed women, who were enjoying, or trying to enjoy, or pretending to enjoy, the "grand masquerade." The scene was gay enough, as novelists say, in all conscience, but it must be confessed that unless one is a member of a large and merry party, or unless one has some particular intrigue to carry to its more or less lurid termination, a masked ball is the deadliest, dullest, dreariest affair that was ever invented for the torture of the long-suffering and ironically so-called "gay world."

On no mind did this circumstance impress itself with drearier persistence than on that of Captain the Honorable Aubyn Goddard, sometime of the Twentieth Hussars, and now occupying the uncomfortable but none the less on that account eagerly-sought-after position of Queen's Messenger.

Captain Goddard was the ideal guardsman of the young lady's dream. Well over the regulation six feet in height, and broad in proportion, his well-balanced head was covered with close-cropped fair hair; his irreproachable moustache was carefully trimmed, and the look of intense boredom on his handsome face gave him a certain Byronic expression that evidently found favor in the majority of bright eyes that flashed from beneath dominos of all colors; or at least so it would seem from the persistency with which the fair—or dark—artillerists attacked him, with nod, beck, wreathed smile, nudge, punch, and apology.

But Captain Aubyn Goddard seemed invulnerable, for no irritation or challenge seemed able to rouse him from his apathy as he leaned against one of the pilasters at the foot of the grand staircase and slightly yawned as he watched the procession before him and wondered vaguely on the chance that found him there when he would infinitely rather be in bed.

I use the word "chance" advisedly.

In his capacity of Queen's Messenger he had arrived in Vienna bearing despatches the previous evening, and early that morning had delivered his despatches at the Austrian Foreign Office. He was to leave on the following afternoon.

For the previous five years the political world had been in a ferment over that time-honored bogie, the Eastern Question. In 1871 Mr. Gladstone had sat calmly in Whitehall, and uttered no protest, whilst Russia, repudiating the Treaty of Paris of 1856, converted the Black Sea into a Russian lake, and the effete demagogue whom Lord Beaconsfield has handed down to posterity in his famous epigram, as "a sophisticated rhetorician inebriated with the exuberance of his own verbosity," had rendered the taking of Sevastopol vain, and surrendered all that Europe had won with her blood in the Crimean War. From that time (1871) a cloud had begun to gather in the East, which now threatened to burst and engulf the Balkan Peninsula, and called forth the historic "Andrassy Note" in December, 1875, following on the rising in Herzegovina.

At the sound of Count Andrassy's clarion, Europe awakened from the sleep into which she had been lulled by successive Liberal governments and Gladstonian croonings, and throughout 1876 there had been almost daily interchange of despatches between London, Berlin, Vienna, and Constantinople. As a natural consequence, trusty messengers were in increased demand, and Captain Aubyn Goddard, having, unlike the majority of men of his years, spent his days as a subaltern in the study of European politics and languages, had been one of the first to receive a commission as one of Her Majesty's postmen, and to commence the nomad career of Queen's Messenger specially detailed for Oriental service.

Things were quieting down, and Europe might have had peace, when the deposition and suicide of Abd-ul-Aziz, and the ten days' sultanate of the imbecile Murad the Fifth, once more gave the malcontents in the Balkan Peninsula the opportunity they had looked for, and brought the present Sultan Abd-ul-Hamid the Second to the throne, determined to put down the disturbances that threatened to rend asunder the empire founded by the first Othman and consolidated by Suleiman the Magnificent.

Some cruelties practised by the Turkish soldiery at Batak in Bulgaria afforded Mr. Gladstone the Irrepressible an opportunity to fulminate which no consideration for the welfare of Europe could allow him to let slip, and accordingly he published his incandescent pamphlet on "Bulgarian Atrocities" that in course of time plunged

Europe in war and gave Russia the opportunity she had so long desired
to encroach in the southeast and southwest of her dominions.

European Cabinets were preparing for the Conference at Constantinople of January, 1877, and thus we find Captain Aubyn Goddard in
Vienna in the August of the preceding year.

As the bearer of important despatches, the Queen's Messenger
had not thought it expedient to look up any of his convivial acquaintances in the Austrian capital, and after delivering his despatches in the
morning he had taken a long and solitary drive, idly wondering how
he should kill the hours of that evening and of the following day
until he should return to the Foreign Office.

On his return from his drive his question was answered for him.
As he entered his hotel an envelope was put into his hand.

He turned it over and over, profoundly perplexed. What could
it mean? Whom could it be from? He had apprised no one
of his arrival, and the handwriting was entirely unfamiliar. But
that he was known was evident; for the superscription was in full:

To—Captain the Honorable Aubyn Goddard.

There was nothing to indicate whether the note was addressed in a
male or a female handwriting: at last he came to the conclusion that
there was only one solution for the mystery, and that that was inside
the envelope.

Accordingly he opened it.

Nothing! not a word of any kind. Only a ticket for the masked
ball at the opera-house that evening.

Well! there was his evening accounted for. But whence could
the ticket have come? Who had brought it? A servant in a black
livery that gave no indication of his master's rank or nationality.

"Anyhow," thought the Queen's Messenger, "I'll go. There
can be no harm in that. I know how to take care of myself. No
doubt my mysterious host will reveal his—or her?—incognito, at the
ball."

And so he had dined, had strolled out on to the Prater and watched
the motley passing panorama of people as he listened to the strains
of "unser Strauss," and when the last chords of the march from
"Tannhäuser" had exploded into the blue vault of the sounding-board
he stepped into a cab and was deposited at the doors of the Grand
Opera-House.

But that had been two hours previous to the moment when we first
set eyes on him, and as yet no solution of the mystery of his presence
there had offered itself. The ball was at its height, and would presently wane. People who had come on business had transacted it and
gone away, people who had come after intrigues had found them and
were developing them, and people who had wandered in, unattached
and for no particular reason, were beginning to have had enough of it
and were turning their thoughts homeward.

Among these latter, as we have said, was the Honorable Aubyn
Goddard, and he had just stretched himself and was casting a last look
round, after the manner of the man who is about to depart, when a
woman passed him.

Her figure, which was gorgeously proportioned, was entirely clad in a tightly-fitting domino of black satin, heavily brocaded with a raised black embroidery. A hood covered her hair, and a black half-mask rendered more brilliant a pair of grand black eyes that caught his for an instant as she passed, and the rich crimson of a rather stern mouth. The jaw was massive, and the complexion colorless. Thus much Goddard had had time to notice, when his attention was diverted to a shambling awkward figure that seemed to be following her. It was that of a man in the costume of a mediæval jester, that accorded well with his sinister, ugly face. As the woman disappeared in the crowd, Goddard saw the hunchback address her, and saw her shrink from him with a gesture of repulsion, leaving him biting his nails as he leered after her for a moment before starting in pursuit.

Captain Goddard for the first time since his arrival felt an awakening interest in the scene, and resumed his place against the pilaster, waiting for the brocaded domino to pass again.

Suddenly he heard an exclamation behind him, and, looking round, saw the same woman hastily descending the grand staircase. At the same moment the hunchback appeared, shuffling down after her, evidently in hot pursuit. He caught her at the foot of the stairs, and as he passed slipped a piece of paper into her hand which she instantly dropped. Next moment both hunchback and domino once more disappeared.

By this time thoroughly aroused, Goddard stooped and picked up the twisted scrap of paper, though not without a certain sensation that he had no right to do so. He opened it.

The paper was blank!

"Egad," said he to himself, "this is getting interesting. But, despatches or no despatches, that little beast mustn't be allowed to insult that glorious creature." And Captain Goddard—who was only a man, after all—started off in the direction the pair had taken.

His towering frame forced for him a passage through the throng, and he had hardly got half-way around before he found himself immediately behind the brocaded domino.

Where was the hunchback? Ah! there he was. He had passed the domino, and was just advancing as if to address her, when the woman turned sharply and was almost thrown into Goddard's arms.

"I beg your pardon," said she in English without a trace of foreign accent, as she stood irresolute before him.

"I beg yours," replied Goddard. "Can I be of any assistance? I see that you are being annoyed."

"If an utter stranger may so far trespass upon the goodness of a gentleman, may I beg you to conduct me to my carriage? I am alarmed and foolishly upset by this man's persecution."

"Certainly," answered Goddard, extending his arm, as he looked round in search of the hunchback, who had disappeared.

Together they made their way to the entrance. Suddenly the woman spoke:

"I beg that you will forgive me, and I hope you will not misunderstand my object in begging your momentary protection, but I felt

that as an English gentleman I could trust you not to look upon me as
—as—one of these."

"Of course; of course," replied Goddard, feeling nevertheless
vaguely disappointed.

They had reached the grand entrance, and Goddard made as if to
turn.

"Not that way," said the domino. "My carriage is at the side-
entrance."

"Oh!" returned the Queen's Messenger, his spirits imperceptibly
reviving.

She led him down a narrow passage to a door that opened upon a
side-street. At the curb stood a perfectly-appointed black coupé, with
a single horse of the same color. Goddard opened the door, and she
stepped in.

"Will you not accept my protection as far as you have to go?" said
Goddard, seeing his "adventure" vanishing into thin air. "You may
not yet be safe."

"No," said she, raising her hand as if to stop him. "I am quite
safe now."

"Can I direct your coachman?"

"He needs no directions."

"At least you will allow me to call and ascertain that you are quite
recovered from your alarm," pleaded Goddard, despairingly.

The woman appeared to reflect for a moment, and then she said,—

"If I give you that permission, will you promise not to make any
inquiries about me, and to forget afterwards that we ever met?"

"Yes,"—this desperately.

"On your honor?"

"On my honor."

"Very well." And she took a card from the rack before her, and
scribbled a word or two on it in pencil, saying, as she handed it to
him, "Do me the pleasure to breakfast with me at this address at
twelve to-morrow, or rather to-day."

"I will be punctual."

"That is well. And now good-night. *Au revoir*, and a thousand
thanks, *Captain Aubyn Goddard!*"

His name! she knew it! He started back to get a better view of
the carriage. Instantly the door was slammed from the inside, and
the coupé dashed off and was lost in the dimly-lighted street.

Goddard took the card which he held in his hand to the nearest
lamp. On it was engraved, in tiny capitals,—

THE BARONESS ALTDORFF,

and an address was added in pencil.

"Well, I'm damned!" remarked Captain Aubyn Goddard to
himself, as he lit a cigar and walked round to the main entrance of the
opera-house as a point of departure for his stroll home in the moonlight.

CHAPTER II.

THE BARONESS ALTDORFF.

NOTWITHSTANDING the late hour of his return from the ball, and the fact that after his return he had spent an hour in fruitless wonder on the events—or rather the event—of the evening, it was a good two hours before mid-day when Captain Aubyn Goddard left his hotel and proceeded to stroll almost unconsciously in the direction of the place of his rendezvous.

To say that he was interested and perplexed is to use a miserably inadequate form of words; but the main outcome of his reflections was that he put the whole thing down as a *bal-masqué* intrigue of a rather more than usual interest, as regarded its commencement at any rate.

There was something indescribably baffling about the woman he had escorted to the street, and whom he hoped to see again within a couple of hours. There was nothing in her voice or manner that betrayed aught but perfect gentleness of birth and breeding. The idea of risking a word of reproof from those wonderful lips, or a look of disdain from those amazing eyes, was quite out of the question; and yet she had made his acquaintance in almost orthodox *bal-masqué* style, and had given him a rendezvous for the morrow in *quite* orthodox *bal-masqué* style. To the Queen's Messenger on service, adventures of all kinds are necessarily a forbidden luxury, and yet Goddard would not for one moment admit to himself that he was running into any personal danger. He could not retrospectively satisfy himself of the woman's nationality. She spoke very perfect English; and yet there was a pretty uncertainty about her *r*'s that betrayed either foreign birth or long residence abroad.

Of the manner of his coming reception, however, he had no doubt. He would be ushered into a boudoir from which daylight would be carefully excluded, a scent of musk or something equally sensuous would hang in the air, the room would be hung with soft silks and decorated with heavily-perfumed exotic flowers, and the woman herself would either be reclining on a divan, or would enter the room with the upward sweep of a shapely arm through velvet portières, clad in some bewitching and lace-covered *négligé*. The woman herself, he felt certain, would be dark, and of a heavy, sensuous type of beauty. The face would be not quite innocent of the *veloutine* of Fay, and would be either of a brilliant coloring or of a properly improper ivory pallor.

Together they would partake of a delicate and *recherché* repast, and after breakfast she would sing to him, accompanying herself on the piano, or more probably on the guitar. And then—— Well, why anticipate?

He was sufficiently "experienced" to know exactly what to expect.

His reflections were suddenly cut short by his arrival at the very house, "The Villa Altdorff," which the *incognita* of the night before had inscribed upon the card she had given him. It was situated quite on the outskirts of the city, where the suburbs begin to assume a distinctly rural appearance. A high quickset hedge divided and hid the grounds of the villa from the road, but a barred gate opened upon a curving drive that led up to the house. A glance at the house did *not* serve to enlighten the Queen's Messenger. It had the appearance of being deserted. All the windows were closed with heavy shutters. No smoke rose from the clustered chimneys, no sign of life appeared within the gate, which was securely fastened.

With difficulty restraining an exclamation of surprise, and forgetting, in his astonishment, his promise not to make inquiries, Goddard turned to a municipal gardener who was sweeping under the tulip-trees that lined the quiet suburban road.

"What is this house?" he asked.

"That," returned the man, eying him suspiciously, "is the Villa Altdorff."

"And who lives here?"

"No one."

"How? No one?"

"No. It has been closed ever since the death of the Baroness Altdorff, three years ago."

"But it does not look neglected."

"No; the family keep the gardens neat, but it is never occupied."

"You are sure?"

The man vouchsafed no answer. He had turned once more to his work, and studiously ignored his questioner, whom he probably took for a gentlemanly burglar compiling notes for a campaign.

So this was the end of his adventure! Better so, after all, thought the Queen's Messenger, since he had to be at the Foreign Office at four to receive Andrassy's despatches. The end? Stay! it wanted yet an hour of mid-day; he would continue his walk and return at the time appointed: at least should chance ever throw him against his dazzling domino again she should not be able to reproach him with not having fulfilled the terms of her invitation.

The Honorable Aubyn Goddard walked on, beyond the outer fortifications.

Punctually at twelve o'clock he found himself once more at the gate of the Villa Altdorff; and now a new surprise awaited him. The gate stood open! He entered. As he walked up the drive he noted with ever-increasing wonderment that the shutters were all thrown open, as were the lower windows. From one chimney a column of smoke rose into the air. On the veranda in front stood two chairs, and some Oriental rugs lay before them. On one of them lay a shawl and a book, giving evidence of recent occupation. From one corner of the rug a very British fox-terrier rose, stretched himself, and trotted down the drive to meet him and assure himself that the perfume of the visitor was a friendly perfume.

As he reached the door it was opened by a grave butler in the correctest black,—not by the pert Parisian maid he had anticipated,—who ushered him at once into a drawing-room matted with Indian grass and furnished throughout in the white-gold style ascribed to Louis XV. Dazed beyond the power of expression, Goddard was walking to a window to inspect the exterior, when the full soft voice that had been echoing in his brain for the past ten hours said behind him,—

"Captain Goddard."

He turned, to see his hostess advancing towards him with outstretched hand.

True to his anticipation, she was dark; but there the correctness of his anticipation began and ended. The gorgeous figure was held with stately erectness, and was clad from throat to foot in the most correctly fitting of tailor-made suits ("Turned out by Morgan, for a fiver!" ejaculated Goddard to himself), at the throat and wrists a collar and cuffs of the snowiest linen, secured by plain gold buttons. Her only ornament was a crimson rose thrust into the bosom of the dress. The raven-black hair was carried smoothly off the high white forehead and drawn to a simple coil at the back of the head.

The vision before him was one of ideal health, perfect womanly beauty, and eminent "good form." Aubyn Goddard stood speechless. The Baroness Altdorff was, of course, perfectly self-possessed.

"You are punctual, Captain Goddard. That is well. We shall have the more time in which to make each other's acquaintance,—or rather to improve it."

"Pardon me," said Goddard, in reply, "if for a few moments I am too bewildered to talk rationally. You have me at a great disadvantage. Will you tell me where we have met before to-day?"

"Not now. But before we part,—yes. Let me see: at four o'clock you must be at the Foreign Office, at five you leave Vienna. I am right, am I not? Yes? Then I propose that we breakfast at once and talk afterwards."

"I am completely at Madame's service."

"Don't make any rash announcements! you ought to mistrust me profoundly. Admit at least that my conduct has been highly irregular."

"Well, I——"

"The fact is," broke in the woman, in a serious tone, "I have long wished to make your acquaintance. The opportunity arrived for me to do you a service, unknown to yourself, and in doing it I killed two birds with one stone: I took the part of Captain Aubyn Goddard in a diplomatic war, and made his acquaintance into the bargain. All is fair, you know, in war!"

"And in love!" concluded Goddard, with a nervous laugh.

"Exactly," replied the Baroness Altdorff, with a slight blush, "but at present the former alone engrosses our attention. But come; breakfast is ready. Will you follow me? Unlike most women who make gentlemen's acquaintances under romantic circumstances, I am ravenously hungry."

She led the way into the dining-room, where a breakfast was served in perfect taste but supreme simplicity.

"At least you will begin," said Goddard, as he seated himself, "by giving me a few words of explanation. First, how did you know my name? and, second, did you send me the ticket for yesterday's ball?"

"I know your name, for in the society of Vienna not to know Captain Aubyn Goddard, of Her Majesty's Diplomatic Service, is to argue one's self unknown. It *was* I who sent you the ticket for last night's ball, for reasons that I will explain to you presently. I am very much interested in the questions that have brought you to Vienna four times in as many months, and chance favored me last night in bringing about a meeting to which I have long looked forward."

She spoke with charming frankness, looking him straight in the eyes, and it was with a, to him, altogether new sensation that he replied, with a little inclination,—

"Whatever may have been your motive, baroness, believe me, I congratulate myself, more profoundly than I can say on so short an acquaintance, on the chance that has thrown us together—at last."

A ring of intense earnestness had come into his voice as he answered, returning her gaze. The woman flushed perceptibly as she turned the conversation:

"Your profession must be a strangely interesting one. You are so much behind the scenes. The Powers will unite in conference about December or January, will they not?"

He glanced at her keenly. "I cannot tell," replied he, cautiously, "but it looks like it at present."

"It seems so strange to me that England should submit so calmly to the dictation of Russia. I should have thought that your government would have despatched a fleet to the Levant."

"That would not take place unless the Conference should prove abortive."

"Ah! then the step is already considered?"

"I do not know," replied Goddard, shortly, as he suddenly perceived that he had been led into an important disclosure. Then he added, "You seem vastly interested in European politics. Ladies do not usually trouble about such matters."

"Oh, I adore them," replied the baroness, with a laugh; "but it annoys me when I see your English interests calmly flung into the lap of Gortschakoff by your Mr. Gladstone."

"Mr. Gladstone will have nothing to do with it," replied Goddard, dryly. "The entertainment of 1871 will not be repeated, I can assure you. So long as Lord Beaconsfield lives, you may be sure that the Pruth will bound Russia on the southwest, and Batoum and Constantinople will *not* become Russian military seaports." He spoke with quick indignation, for Goddard was of the true Tory faith, and the light tone of this foreign woman stung him in a sensitive place. The Baroness Altdorff plunged her eyes deep into his, and leaned forward as she replied,—

"That is how I like to hear a man talk. *That* is the substance of your despatches, on this mission?"

Goddard was about to lie promptly in expressing his ignorance, but something in the woman's look made his heart leap into his throat, and he answered nothing, as the color rose to the roots of his hair.

"That is right," she said, softly. "I could not imagine you lying to me."

"No," answered the man, shortly : "I cannot lie to you."

The Baroness Altdorff rose.

"Let us go into the drawing-room," she said, with a sudden change of manner. "We have yet an hour before you need start. At half-past three my coupé will take you to the Foreign Office, and thence to the station. Will you oblige me by sending my man from the Office to settle your bill and bring your luggage from your hotel? I do not want you to return."

"Really, I feel ashamed to take advantage——" began Goddard.

"Promise me! promise me!" she interrupted, eagerly.

"Certainly, it shall be as you wish. But, in heaven's name, give me some explanation of all this mystery."

"Very well," replied she ; "I will. I need not tell Captain Goddard that diplomacy in Russia sticks at nothing. I happened to have learnt that an effort would be made to detain you in Vienna by the Russian agents there. You were to be summoned from your hotel last night. They laid their plans well. I sent you the ticket to insure your absence, and came myself to the ball to see that you were safely there. The hunchback whom you saw persecuting me adopted that course to mix you up in a most unpleasant *esclandre*. He knew that an English gentleman would not suffer an unprotected woman to be insulted in his presence. It is needless to say that he was a political spy. Had we left the opera-house by the main entrance you would have found yourself this morning in a duel or a police court. It was necessary to hide you to-day. I thought of this place as we sought my carriage. They have watched for you at your hotel all day. Remember, you have promised not to return there with your despatches."

"Do you think I am going to run away from the creature?" said Goddard, indignantly.

"It is your duty to guard your despatches," answered the woman, calmly.

"You are right," answered he, simply, after a pause.

The conversation took another turn. Her interest drew from Goddard—almost, I was going to say, the story of his life, and when the clock struck half-past three it was almost with a start that he recalled himself to the present.

It was the Baroness Altdorff who cut the conversation short. "It is time for you to go," she said. "I am sorry."

"And I too, baroness," replied Goddard. "I have not half expressed to you my gratitude for all you have done for me, still less for these charming hours with you."

"Then you forgive my plot against your liberty?"

"Yes," replied he, boldly. "All is fair, as we said, in love and war, and—and both are here."

The Baroness Altdorff crimsoned despite herself.

"Good-by," said she, holding out her hand again.

"Not good-by, I trust," pleaded he, as he held the delicate white hand in his. They had reached the front door, where the presence of the grave butler holding open the door of the coupé which stood in readiness placed a restraint upon the wild declaration he was tempted to pour out to her. "Not good-by, baroness, but *au revoir*. Is it not so?" And he leaned forward as he pressed the taper fingers.

"I hope so,—believe me," replied she, and her pallor intensified.

"Then I go not altogether in despair," said Goddard, gayly, as he descended the steps.

As he took his seat in the carriage he turned to where she stood on the veranda.

"I forgot!" he exclaimed. "You said you would tell me where we met before to-day. Where was it?"

"At the ball last night."

The servant slammed the door, and the carriage whirled off down the drive. As it turned out of the gate, Goddard looked hastily out of the window. The windows of the Villa Altdorff were once more shuttered as they had been in the morning. No smoke rose from the chimneys. All signs of human habitation had disappeared.

The Villa Altdorff seemed deserted!

Captain the Honorable Aubyn Goddard flung himself back on the cushions of the coupé.

"By Jove!" he exclaimed, "this carriage is real enough, or I should believe the whole thing was a dream."

* * * * * * * *

Whilst he transacted his business at the Foreign Office, the coupé went to his hotel for his luggage.

The servant brought back word that two gentlemen refusing to give their names had been waiting for him since mid-day.

They were waiting still.

CHAPTER III.

THE POWER BEHIND THE THRONE.

THE police system of Russia is divided into three sections, the First Section, consisting of the ordinary patrol of *gendarmerie*, the Second Section, consisting of what are called the Political Police, originally instituted by the Tzar Nicholas to control corruption among officials, but now, and at the time of which I write, a vast organization having its representatives in almost every city of the world, and the hated and dreaded Third Section, of Secret Police, having its spies in every house, in every restaurant, in every public place, almost in every family. The three are united under one head, and during the crisis of 1876–77 that head had, as may be supposed, more than enough to occupy it.

One of the largest suites in the Public Offices of Petersburg is devoted to the Ministry of Foreign Affairs. Adjoining it is the Ministry of the Interior. Connecting the two are two small rooms, one an inner room opening upon the vestibule, the other looking out upon the Newski Prospect. These two rooms are devoted to the use of the Chief of Police—"The White Terror," as he is called—and his personal staff, consisting of a private and two ministerial secretaries.

In the outer room sat Prince Schouloff, the Chief of Police, and the position he occupied between the two principal Ministries indicated his importance in the affairs of the Empire.

No one who saw him seated in his great leather-covered chair before his table could fail to be impressed with the personality of the man. Though he sits huddled up, as it were, there can be no mistaking the massive proportions of the man : his hand alone, as it lies on the table before him, gives overwhelming evidence of his tremendous physical strength. He is a comparatively young man,—not more than forty years old,—despite the fact that his closely-cut hair is almost snow-white, and that the clearly-traced lines round his eyes and mouth give evidence of years of anxiety, if not of physical suffering. In startling contrast to his white hair are his thick eyebrows and elaborately-pointed moustache, which are of the intensest black. At this moment his keen gray eyes look straight before him from beneath the heavy brows, and his face wears the expression habitual to it in repose,—one of concentrated watchfulness.

Before him—it is morning—lies a heap of letters, which for the past half-hour has been slowly diminishing as he opens one after another, and, after making a note upon each in pencil, for the direction of the secretaries, lays them in two heaps, one to the right of the pile for the political secretaries, the other to the left for future private reference. At this moment the morning task of looking through the mail has been arrested,—arrested by the paper that he holds in the hand that lies on the desk before him. He is not looking at it. It would be useless, for it is not of an ordinary kind. It is written on a large square sheet of thin blue paper; in the upper left-hand corner, arranged within a diamond, appears the following design, in Greek capitals :

Incomprehensible to the uninitiated, Prince Schouloff reads within the lozenge the word "Bella-Demonia. A.II.2.R.", and, having progressed thus far, he has laid down the paper and is plunged in thought. The letter is in cipher, and is sealed to him until the arrival of his private secretary, who has the custody of the key to the enigma.

He has not long to wait. A slight noise behind him causes him to turn his head. A young man has entered the room, and has silently taken his seat at a smaller desk in the corner.

"Ah, Dmitri Dmitrievitch, is that you? I am waiting for you."

"A despatch from Bella-Demonia?"

"Yes. Have you your dial?"

"Here it is, Excellency."

"Set it: A.H.2.R."

"It is done."

"Read me this." And the Chief of Police hands the document to his private secretary, and turns once more to the unopened letters before him. For half an hour no sound breaks the silence, save the slight squeak of the cipher-dial, as, letter by letter, the young man interprets the despatch.*

---

* BELLA-DEMONIA'S CIPHER-DIAL.

The cipher-dial referred to in the text, the original of which is in my possession, is an instrument of great interest and ingenuity, and an explanatory note may not be out of place at this point. It is a mode of cipher-construction that practically defies solution, like a combination-lock, and was used by the staff in command of the forces in Asia Minor during the Turko-Russian War, on whose main outlines the story of Bella-Demonia has been constructed.

All that is necessary, for two people who wish to communicate in cryptograph by its means, to bear in mind is a key or combination, such as is used by Bella-Demonia in the text,—to wit, A.H.2.R.

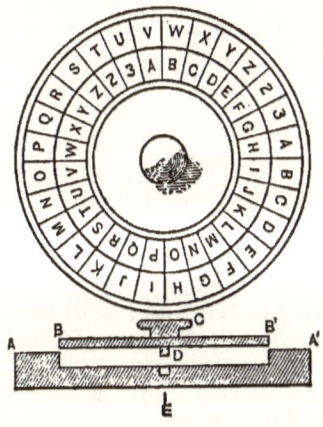

The instrument consists of an outer dial, AA', out of which a circular chamber has been cut which receives a smaller dial, BB', which falls into its place so as to be level with the raised rim of the dial AA'. It is further kept in place by a little pin, D, which falls into a hole in the centre of the dial AA', as at E. The dial BB' may be rotated from the dial AA' by means of the milled knob C. The alphabet and a few numerals are engraved round the edges of the dials, as seen in the illustration.

Now, supposing Bella-Demonia to be writing the despatch referred to above, on the combination A.H.2.R. She sets the dial as in the illustration. The H of the inner circle falls under the A of the outer. The "2R" means that the dial BB' must be rotated two spaces to the right, to find each letter in the cryptograph message. "1R" would mean, one space to the right; "3L," three to the left, and so on.

We will assume that Bella-Demonia wishes to write her own name on the formula A.H.2.R. The dial is set as in the illustration.

She turns the dial BB' to the right, so as to find the second space from the B in the upper or outer circle (of the dial AA'). It will be found that the letter that falls under B is G. G, therefore, is the first letter. Now to find the equivalent of the second, E; without moving the dials she finds E in the outer circle, turns the dial BB' two spaces to the right, and finds the letter H has come under the E. H is therefore the second letter of the word Bella-Demonia. Next the L. L is found on the outer dial, the inner is revolved two spaces, and M is the letter found. Now for the second L. The dial BB' is once more shifted two to the right, and the letter K represents the second L. Following the rule, and always turning the dial two spaces to the right, A is found on the outer and in turn Z on the inner circle, so that the letters GHMKZ represent the word BELLA; and, proceeding in the same way, DEMONIA is represented in cryptograph by the letters 2.Z.D.D.A.V.L.

BELLADEMONIA=GHMKZ2ZDDAVL.

Now, Prince Schouloff *receives* the letters Ghmkz2zddavl, and to find out what they mean sets *his* dial A.H.2.R.,—*i.e.*,with the A of the dial AA' over the H of the dial BB'.

In *reading*, the above process is reversed *only* in the fact that the *letter to be interpreted* is sought on the inner circle (of the dial BB'). He finds G on the dial BB', rotates it two spaces to the right, and finds over it, on the dial AA', the letter B. Next he rotates the H on BB', and finds over it E on AA'. The M on BB' rotated

At the end of that time the secretary rises and lays before his chief a paper on which appears the following, in French:

"VIENNA, 25th August, 1876.

"Captain the Honorable Aubyn Goddard, Twentieth Hussars, especially detailed Queen's Messenger for Oriental affairs. Age about 34. Single. English gentleman in every sense of the word. Unapproachable by ordinary means. Passed through Vienna August 15 and 16, bearing despatches for Foreign Office.

"In the event of Conference, England will maintain armed neutrality. In the event of Russia taking meditated action, will occupy the Bosphorus. Integrity of Ottoman Empire will be supported : particular attention to Batoum and Trebizonde. No further details.

"Leave for Petersburg to-night.

"BELLA-DEMONIA."

"H'm!" ejaculated the Chief of Police, as he carefully folded the cipher message and its translation and placed them in his pocket-book. "This is important. 'English gentleman. Unapproachable by ordinary means. No further details.' I don't like that. Bella-Demonia does not usually stop half-way in her inquiries. She is coming here. That is well, and I shall meet this marvellous woman at last!"

And, the current of his thoughts evidently changed by the receipt of the despatch, he altered some of the notes on the letters before him, and as one of the secretaries took away the bundle for distribution he said to him,—

"Inform the secretary of His Excellency the Minister for War that Prince Schouloff will wait upon his Chief in an hour's time."

When this latter had left the room, the prince turned to Dmitri Dmitrievitch Keratieff, his private secretary, and remarked,—

"You are sure that you never heard your father, Dmitri Keratieff, refer by name to this Baroness Altdorff,—'Bella-Demonia,' as they call her?"

"Never, Excellency. After the attempt upon the life of His Majesty in which my father received his death-wound, he spoke to me

two spaces gives him L on AA'; and K on BB' rotated two spaces gives him a second L. Z treated the same way gives A on AA', and thus out of "Ghmkz" the first half " Bella" is produced, and in the same way the whole word, and the whole despatch.

The great point to be noted is that by this means the same letter never means the same thing twice, so that the principal means of deciphering cryptograms—*i.e.*, the observation of the most recurrent letters and substituting for them the commonest vowels and consonants—is destroyed. Without ever going more than two spaces to the right or left, 4010 different combinations can be formed; whilst if the persons in possession of the dials choose to read *upward* for writing and *downward* for reading, instead of as above *downward* for writing and *upward* for reading, 16,080,100 combinations can be formed, and it is that number of chances to one against anybody but the right person hitting on the formula.

Of course any arrangement of the letters of the alphabet, and any number of numerals, omitting the 1 and the 0, can be engraved on the two dials, so long as they coincide exactly with each other.

SELINA DOLARO.

of a woman who possessed his cipher-dial, but never mentioned her name. I was very young then."

At the private secretary's words Prince Schouloff's face clouded. The attempted assassination of the Tzar in which the late Chief of Police lost his life was a subject which the present Chief—for state reasons, he said—never allowed to be mentioned in his presence. However, his private secretary, as son of his predecessor, and Prince Schouloff's especial *protégé*, considered himself a privileged person. At the time of his father's death Dmitri Dmitrievitch Keratieff had been one of the junior clerks in the Department of Police, and when his father met his death in the abortive attempt of the followers of Alexis Dorski, Prince Schouloff, who came to Petersburg to take the direction of the police, sought out his predecessor's son and appointed him his confidential secretary. Dorski had disappeared,—he was reported killed at Odessa soon after,—and his society had been broken up. From that moment his conspiracy had been a forbidden subject, like many others, in the Department of Police.

Now, however, the Chief did not silence his secretary, but remarked, with the air of a man who dimly recalls a half-forgotten incident,—

"How did he refer to her?"

"Though it was eight years ago, I remember his words as if they had been spoken yesterday. 'Dmitri,' he said, 'you are too young now to understand the workings of the section in which you are a subordinate; but some day you may be called to a position of trust therein. There exists a duplicate of the cipher-dial with which I construct my political correspondence. Should ever a woman communicate with you by its means, lay the matter at once before your Chief, and tell him that I, Dmitri Keratieff, left for him the injunction that she was to be considered. Trust her utterly: the welfare of the Holy Russian Empire is in her heart, and may be in her hands.' I believe this Bella-Demonia to be the woman, Excellency, for my father would never have intrusted his cipher-dial to any one who would either duplicate or misuse it."

"I think you are right," returned Schouloff, as he reconcentrated his attention upon the papers before him.

That day he devoted to important interviews with the Ministers of War and of Foreign Affairs, and at the closing of the office at four o'clock another step, and an important one, had been taken in the policy that was to eventuate in the war of 1877.

The office was closed. The secretaries had gone, a servant had placed a reading-lamp upon his table, and Prince Schouloff was alone.

He stretched his arms above his head in the manner of a man concluding his work or turning to some lighter employment. No one looking at him as he sat, idly for the moment looking out over the Prospect that teemed with life below him, would have dreamed that the hard, ascetic-looking man, with "diplomacy" written on every line of his face, the man whose word could at any moment send families to Siberia with a "wolf's passport," or plunge the Cabinet in international complications, had been, eight years before we see him in the office of the Police—Alexis Dorski, the Nihilist!

It was he. But of this circumstance only two living souls were aware, and those were Prince Schouloff himself—and in after-years, people who know have said, *One other.*

CHAPTER IV.

BELLA-DEMONIA.

PRINCE Schouloff rose, and, walking to the window, looked out over the Prospect of Alexander Newski, seeking a momentary relief from the cramped position to which he had been constrained by his work during the hours of toil. For a few minutes he stood idly watching the droschkies and troïkas that crossed and recrossed one another, listening to the jangle of their bells and to the vague murmur of the *isvoshtshiks'* voices as they apostrophized and harangued their ponies, after the manner of their class. Then he drew down the blinds to shut out the remainder of the already dying daylight, and seated himself once more at his bureau.

From a carefully-locked drawer he took a small bundle of folded blue sheets, and placed at the bottom thereof " Bella-Demonia's" despatch of the morning, and was about to replace the bundle, when a second thought struck him, and he unfolded them all in turn, running his eyes rapidly over their contents as he did so. All the originals were in cipher, but the translation was attached to each in his secretary's handwriting.

"This is a most marvellous woman," soliloquized he, as he concluded his cursory examination of the bundle. " I wonder how she is to be accounted for. Among all the political agents of the Russian administration, of her alone nothing is known: as a rule, the Holy Empire is well informed as to the antecedents of its—spics; but in the case of this woman it is different. Who is she?—or, rather, who was she? Who is—or was—the Baron Altdorff? I have sent Dmitri Keratieff in turn to London, Berlin, Paris, Vienna, in search of information regarding her. I have inquired into all her aliases in vain: everywhere we are met and assisted by her work, but by the woman herself —never. Well, well, notwithstanding the mystery, I would trust her where I would not trust Dmitri Keratieff himself. The treasury of the Department has been at her service for five years. A mere adventuress—my English agent Emily Dashton, for instance—in her position would long ago have realized a million or so of roubles and disappeared. But Bella-Demonia is true to her trust under all circumstances: her motive, whatever it be, must be a strong one, and in due time no doubt she will elect to present herself. She says in this last despatch that she is coming here: when will she arrive? By St. Nicholas! I—I, Schouloff, confess that I am curious—nay, anxious—to see her.—What is it?"

The concluding words of his soliloquy were addressed to the

dvornik of the office, who had entered the room after a premonitory knock.

"A lady," replied the *dvornik*, "desires to speak with your Excellency." And he handed to the prince a card on which was engraved "The Countess Laroche, Avenue de Jena, Paris," and in pencil had been added, in Russian, "Hôtel d'Europe,—*Evropeiskaya Gosstinnitza.*"

"You told her that the office was closed?"

"Yes, Excellency, but she insisted that I should inquire if you were still here."

"Did she state her business?"

"No, Excellency: she said only that she had just arrived from Vienna."

"From Vienna? Ah! Admit her, and order two of the guard to station in the secretaries' office, before she comes through it."

Prince Schouloff had twice narrowly escaped assassination in this very room, and was prepared for emergencies.

Two minutes later a woman entered the room. She stood for a moment at the door, and said, interrogatively,—

"Prince Schouloff?"

"I am he," returned Schouloff, scrutinizing her narrowly. "Be seated, *sodaini.*" He spoke in Russian, and his visitor answered in the same language:

"I see you have placed your Cossacks in the anteroom. I should have saved you the trouble by announcing myself as the Baroness Altdorff. It suits me, however, to be the Countess Laroche, travelling for her health: so I gave to the *dvornik* the name by which I am to be known so long as I remain in Petersburg." There was a simple, commanding dignity in her words as she spoke, seating herself the while in the chair indicated, opposite to the Chief of Police. Prince Schouloff had remained standing.

"Bella-Demonia!" he said, simply.

"I am she."

Without another word, he went to the door, and called out, "*Choroskho! Ogon!*" ("All right! Go away!") and the footsteps of the two soldiers were heard retiring down the corridor. Schouloff returned, and, seating himself in the great leather-covered chair, remarked,—

"I will not waste time in trivial compliments. I can only say that it affords me a profound satisfaction to meet Bella-Demonia face to face. You will explain the object of this visit in your own words and at your own time."

"It was time for us to meet. The negotiations at Vienna are practically closed. You will find that Bismarck and Andrassy are acting together, have done so from the first, and will do so to the end. The policy of Great Britain is cut and dried. Their plans are formed. It is time to form ours."

"Ours?"

"Yes,—yours and mine."

Schouloff thought for a moment. Then he said,—

"Madame von Altdorff, let us understand each other from the commencement——"

"Countess Laroche, if you please," corrected she.

"Very good,—Countess Laroche. You are staying at the Hôtel d'Europe. Have you a passport?—but of course you have."

"I have five," returned she, simply.

"I beg your pardon!"

"Here they are," said she, taking a thin packet from the bosom of her dress. "Two of them are, as you see, countersigned by yourself. Here is that of the Countess Laroche, dated, issued, and visa-ed in Paris; these are respectively those of Mrs. Damian, issued and visa-ed in London; of the Baroness Altdorff, signed by yourself, in Berlin; of the Baroness Altdorff, similarly signed, in Vienna; and of Madame Raczewitz, issued, and so forth, in Constantinople."

The Chief of Police seemed thunderstruck.

"Madame," said he, "in two minutes you have impressed me as I have never been impressed before. May I ask your nationality? Your Russian is perfect, but foreign; your French is the same."

"I am cosmopolitan. I am in turn English, French, German, Russian, and, what is most to our present purpose, Roumeliote, but always and everywhere Bella-Demonia. Do I make myself clear?"

"To me—perfectly. Your identity established, pray consider the Department of Police at your service. And now, what have you to say?"

"More than can be said now. One question, however, before we terminate this interview. When do we declare war?"

Schouloff started, despite his training, despite himself.

"War?" he echoed.

"Yes,—with Turkey."

For reply the Chief leaned forward and raised the shade from the lamp, flooding the room with light. He fixed his eyes on Bella-Demonia's face. She returned his gaze unflinchingly. She was dressed from head to foot in some black-beaded material, with here and there a flash of crimson, in a lining, a ribbon, or a feather. The Chief was apparently satisfied with his scrutiny.

"When the Porte shall have rejected the conditions presented by the Conference."

"They will not be of a nature that the Porte *can* accept?"

A moment's pause, and then Schouloff answered, shortly,—

"No!"

"Good! That is enough for to-day. To-morrow I will lay *my* plans before you. Is it agreed?"

"Perfectly."

Ten minutes later Prince Schouloff sat alone in his sanctum, buried in his complicated reflections.

CHAPTER V.

A PLAN OF CAMPAIGN.

On the following afternoon, when the secretaries had gone and the offices had been closed to the world, as the bells of the neighboring Cathedral of St. Isaac's tolled the hour of five, Prince Schouloff sat once more in his sanctum, in conference with the Baroness Alt-dorff.

"As I understand the position," Bella-Demonia was saying, "our plans stand thus. The conditions laid before the Ottoman Cabinet will be of a nature that will render their acceptance impossible. When this is an accomplished fact, and the Powers have protested by protocol, Russia will cross the Pruth, and enter Asia Minor by Batoum or Kars without further notice."

"Exactly."

"What opposition shall we meet?"

"In Europe, little or none. Roumania will join our cause, and probably Bulgaria. In Asia we shall probably have difficulty with Moukhtar Pasha."

"And where shall we station our political observatory?"

"Probably at Odessa."

"That is wrong. It is too far from Stamboul."

"Has Bella-Demonia anything better to suggest?"

"Certainly, or she would not be here. Give me a map of the country."

Schouloff laid a chart of the Balkan Peninsula on the table, and together they bent over the sheet, the woman demonstrating with her finger as she spoke quickly and decisively, in the tones of one stating a case with which he is entirely familiar:

"Immediately on the declaration of war, long before we reach the Danube, the Buda-Pesth, Giurgevo, and Varna route to Constantinople will be closed. The ports of the Black Sea will be blockaded, the sea-route from any other port will be impracticable. The only line of communication between the Powers and the Porte, therefore, will be across the Balkans by way of the Shipka Pass. To reach this point, messengers must pass through Belgrade, Widin, and possibly Plevna. From Shipka they must reach Stamboul by Eski Saghra and Adrian-ople. On the road between the two lies the village of Deve-kini. At that village Madame Helen Raczewitz, a Roumeliote lady, must take a hunting-villa at once. By the time our armies cross the Pruth she will be firmly established there, and his Excellency Prince Schouloff will always be a welcome visitor."

As she ceased she looked up into Schouloff's face to mark the effect of her words.

"Then you propose——" said he.

"To found a political observatory, away from large cities or military centres, though within a certain radius of Eski Saghra,—an observatory, however, on the inevitable line of route between Stamboul and Europe."

"But between this and next year I have important duties that call me to Paris and London. I could not occupy the château of which you speak."

"But I could. I propose to be there within a month."

"You know the state of a civilized country on the first outbreak of a war and before military control is established. Do you fully realize what would be the condition of affairs in Bulgaria? The good

Gladstone was nearer the truth than is his wont in his *brochure* on Batak."

Bella-Demonia's lip curled scornfully.

"Do you think," said she, "that a woman who has lived the life of Bella-Demonia is likely to flinch at the thought of a sojourn in a country notoriously Russophile? Besides, inquire at Philippopolis and Sofia concerning Madame Raczewitz: you will be satisfied, I think, that I am safe among the Balkans."

Prince Schouloff had resumed his seat, and now remained silent for a few moments, watching the woman opposite him.

"Madame von Altdorff," said he, at length, "I do not ask a confidence which apparently you are desirous of withholding, but it is obvious that it must have been some terrible cataclysm in your life that plunged you into the whirlpool of political intrigue."

"A cataclysm indeed!—one that shattered every womanly feeling within me; one that turned my life into one protracted longing for excitement and distraction. When, on the death of Dmitri Keratieff at the hands of Alexis Dorski's band, *you* took his place in the councils of the nation, a month of keen observation of your methods satisfied me that under your chieftainship the office of political agent would be no sinecure. I wrote to you: you gave me my first commission, and in an hour my womanhood, my past, was laid aside,—in a word, I became—Bella-Demonia!"

"I would that we had met sooner, baroness. With such a partner as yourself, there is no height to which an ambitious man might not aspire."

She looked at him for an instant as if in alarm. Then, resuming the cold, hard tone that was natural to her, she said,—

"It is just as well that we did not meet then, for I am incapable of aught but hate. You understand me?"

"Perfectly," replied Schouloff. And the conversation changed.

A fortnight later the "plan of campaign" was settled. Day after day the Chief of Police had been closeted with the Baroness Altdorff, and nothing remained to be discussed, of the policy of the Chief and his *lieutenante.* "The Countess Laroche" was making ready for her departure; and in two days' time Prince Schouloff would have left Petersburg for Paris *en route* for London.

They sat, as usual, in the bureau of the Department of Police, and Bella-Demonia had just folded up her last sheet of notes, written in the cipher under which we first made her acquaintance.

"So!" she said, "all is finished."

"Almost," replied Schouloff.

"How? almost? Have you anything else to say?"

"Yes. Give me your attention, if you please, for a few moments longer, baroness: what remains to be said is not unimportant." He paused for a moment, as if searching for words: then he resumed. "You have never enlightened me, baroness, on the subject of your past, and for my part I have no desire to be enlightened. I only know that you are incomparable as you are incomprehensible; I only know that, whatever your birth may have been, you would add lustre to any name that you would deign to adopt. The family of Schouloff is second to none in the Russian Empire, and since before our history began the Schouloffs have ranked side by side with the Romauoffs, the Dolgouroukis, and the Khristovs. This name, in all humility, I offer to you. Will you be my wife?"

Bella-Demonia had risen and walked to the window.

There, she turned and faced Schouloff, who sat, nervously—for him—twisting an end of his moustache.

"Prince Schouloff," said she, "I regret from the bottom of my soul that you should have honored me with this proposition. I can never be more to you than I am now. I know that I am in your power, I have expressed my willingness to place myself still further in your hands, and I have no fear for the result. But more than your adjutant I can never be. Let us forget this scene, and resume our old positions with regard to each other. I can *never* be your wife."

A sharp contraction passed across the man's features, but he regained his old icy composure as he replied,—

"I know you too well to urge my suit. Some day I hope, however, that you may reconsider your decision. Should that day ever arrive, I leave it in your hands to tell me of it. Meanwhile, I am always your obedient servant."

She inclined her head in silence.

"I think there is no more to be said," he resumed. "So, *au revoir.* Early in the year I will join you in our Bulgarian observatory."

"Good!" she replied, simply. "I shall look forward to your coming. *Au revoir!*"

BOOK II.

CHAPTER I.

A COMMITTEE OF WAYS AND MEANS.

"But, my dear girl, for heaven's sake be reasonable. How the deuce do you suppose I can get ten thousand pounds?"

"How should I know?"

"Very well, then : don't be absurd."

And Major Homer Carteret and Mrs. Bradley Dashton sat looking at each other as if hoping to derive inspiration from each other's ingenuous countenances.

They were excellently well matched, this brother and sister : he was a gentlemanly adventurer, and she was a garrison hack. This is perhaps a trifle crude. Let us explain.

Major Homer Carteret was "society runner" for a syndicate of Oriental gentlemen who promoted companies in the far-Eastern city. His was the task of snaring ornamental directors with high-sounding titles, and moneyed youngsters with plethoric bank-accounts : no one in the business had so keen a scent or so sure a hand, no one was so innocent a (professional) victim or so enthusiastic a (professional) supporter as Major Homer Carteret, and, though Dick Saville and other ribald spirits who had suffered by and with him averred that his military commission· was one in the Salvation Army, there was no denying that, diplomatic and deprecating to the last degree, Major Carteret was a most useful member of the society which for a consideration he adorned.

To explain yet further, the major owed his rank to some obscure Indian regiment, and according to his own account had seen much service in the Empire; but a majority in a Sikh regiment is not a lucrative post, nor is it one in which the undoubted talents of the major found full scope, and he took the first opportunity to seek the mother-country as the pioneer of a queer gold-mining company, and, having found the work profitable and congenial, realized that *this* was his proper sphere, and settled in London, where his fame spread among wealthy but unpresentable financiers, as purveyor of directors and social "drummer" for the stocks of his employers. His business found an able co-operator in the person of his sister, when she too forsook her all—to wit, all the officers in Bengal—and established herself in the cosey little house in Mayfair where we find her sitting on this bright November morning, in conference with Major Homer Carteret.

Their tactics were such as to compel the admiration of all who suffered by them. The major and his sister were "devilish good fellows," both of them : did any gilded youth desire to meet any particular damsel *en petit comité*, Mrs. Dashton could always be depended upon to give a little dinner, at which she and her brother counted for little save as hosts. During dinner Mrs. Dashton, with some excuse or apology for talking shop, would deftly draw from the major a few enthusiastic words regarding his last "investment;" over the wine and the first cigar the major generally managed to re-introduce the subject, and the gilded youth, as a rule, bit at the bait and "went a hundred" in company with the major, "just for fun." The company generally turned out to be one of unlimited liability, and in due season burst with more or less explosive force, and the major when reproached would express the most awful consternation, but "as a friend of the directors" would manage to limit the gilded youth's liability to a "few" thousands, whilst he, poor old ·chap, was absolutely ruined, and in his despair would borrow five hundred for a month to get himself on his feet again. As the five hundred was always punctually repaid, he always got it, and with it the commiseration and absolution of his unconscious victims. For the supply of ornamental directors he had a fixed ascending scale : a baronet, so much ; a baron, so much ; a viscount, an earl, a marquis, a duke, so much apiece, according to the standing of the title in the financial Debrett which financiers keep locked up in their strong boxes.

For her share in the proceedings Mrs. Dashton charged a regular commission, with now and then a bonus. At this moment she wanted a bonus, but the bonus she wanted was ten thousand pounds, and at this moment it was decidedly inconvenient. The major was "filling the cast," to put it dramatically, of a company for the exploitation of some absolutely inaccessible copper-mines in Asia Minor, and, though the syndicate was wealthy, the major had run through about as much " petty cash" as the concern could stand.

He was consequently constrained to remark,—

" For heaven's sake, be reasonable !"

" Well, it's your own affair, Homer. If Arlingford doesn't have this ten thou. by Monday, ' up he goes' at Tattersall's and the Club; and that means the extinction of Arlingford ; and the extinction of Arlingford means the extinction of the Ararat Mining Company."

" But, hang it all, he's had between fifteen and twenty thousand already, and the company is beginning to look into the accounts."

" Well, what if he has? you've had the value of your money. Without his house for head-quarters you'd never have filled your board of directors, and you certainly wouldn't have got young Saville, or young Midas, to ' go a hundred for fun,' as you call it. Besides, you *must* get this American Briggs. He's a millionaire, and so long as Arlingford's on his feet you can always strike him there. He's to be at this dinner there to-night to say good-by to Goddard."

" Goddard ?"

" You argue yourself unknown. Twentieth Hussars, Queen's Messenger, most popular man in London."

" Never met him."

" No, you wouldn't ; he hasn't got any hundreds ' to go for fun'."

" Keep to business, if you please."

" I *am* keeping to business. I want ten thousand pounds."

" Well, I haven't got them, and can't get them. There."

" Well, what are we going to do ?"

" I don't know. Can't you borrow it from Schouloff? These Russian princes are always fabulously rich."

" Schouloff could certainly get it me if he wanted anything in return for it. He told me at the Ackerlys' last night that there was a favor I could do him ; but I can't do him ten thousand pounds' worth of work in three days."

" Still, you could try him. See what he wants."

" I shall certainly do that this afternoon ; but it's a forlorn hope."

There was a minute's silence, and then the brother broke out :

" Don't sit saying nothing ! Suggest something, for goodness' sake."

" I was just about to do so," returned Mrs. Dashton, her eyes fixed on the fire. " You go straight into the city and move heaven and earth to get the money. I'll write to Schouloff to get him here this afternoon. Write from the city to Lady Arlingford to say you are detained, but will come in after dinner : I'll write later on and say I'm ill, but will also come in afterwards. Meet me at Arlingford's at nine o'clock, and before they're out from dinner we'll compare notes. I haven't much hope."

" Nor have I."

" Well, do your best, anyhow."

" You bet I will."

And Major Homer Carteret took up his hat and left the house.

As soon as he had gone, Mrs. Bradley Dashton sat down and wrote a few lines.

"Take this," said she to the servant who appeared in answer to her summons, "to the Russian Legation, and wait for an answer."

This done, she walked to the fire and held out her fingers to the blaze.

Mrs. Bradley Dashton was an extremely handsome woman in the luxurious blonde style of beauty. Her eight-and-twenty years sat lightly on her fuzzy brow, and the ravages of the Indian climate, and the excitement of her life as the successive flame of every subaltern in the Bengal Staff Corps, had left no trace upon her regular features.

This had not escaped the notice of the Earl of Arlingford when he visited India on a hunting-tour, a couple of years before, and, unmindful of the existence of his wife in England, or perhaps relying on that lady for protection against the ultimate wiles of the siren, he had easily persuaded her to abandon Bengal for London; and in her secret soul Emily Dashton cherished a hope, founded on a light promise of Lord Arlingford's, that so soon as her ladyship should seek redress of her wrongs through the medium of the divorce court, she, Emily Dashton, should graduate as the Countess of Arlingford in the peerage of England.

Hence her anxiety to aid his lordship in the present strait, hence her late conference with her brother the major, and hence her summons to Prince Schouloff, whose ally she had been, off and on, ever since her return to England.

The answer to the latter arrived promptly, and with a little sigh of satisfaction Mrs. Bradley Dashton proceeded to lunch.

CHAPTER II.

A POLITICAL COMMISSION.

At three o'clock that afternoon, clad in the most bewitching of wrappers, Mrs. Bradley Dashton lay curled up in an arm-chair before her fire, expectant. It cannot be said that her features were free from care, for there's many a slip 'twixt the fingers and ten thousand pounds; still, she was more hopeful than she had been in the morning, for Schouloff's prompt reply to her note and his obedience to her summons pointed to the fact that there was something she could do for him, and Prince Schouloff's service, though one of danger and intricacy, was excellently well paid.

The miniature cathedral chimes of the carriage-clock on the mantel-piece had hardly struck thrice when Mrs. Dashton heard a hansom checking its mad career at her door, and, a moment after, Schouloff entered the room. She did not rise, but extended to him her hand, which the Russian bent himself reverentially to kiss.

"And how goes it with my charming ally?" he began.

"Pretty well, thanks. At this moment I'm bored. I want something to do,—something exciting. That's why I asked you to call."

"Ah! I thought as much. Well, how much is it this time?" he asked, in a matter-of-fact tone of voice.

"Ten thousand pounds."

" Dear me! is that all ?"

" That's all for the present," said she, ignoring the sarcasm.

" *Only* ten thousand pounds!" repeated Prince Schouloff.

" Can I have it ?"

" Well, I hope so. It will depend on yourself."

" You don't mean to say," she said, eagerly, " that there's anything I can do for you that's worth ten thousand pounds? I want it by Monday."

" If you will do what I want, your work will be done by midnight. At one A.M., unless you fear I might compromise you by so untimely a call, I will come here and pay you ten thousand pounds, in notes or gold. How do you want them ?"

" Don't play with me, Schouloff," said the woman, nervously : " I can't bear it. I want this money awfully badly."

" I am not playing. I was never more serious in my life. I heard that his lordship needed ten thousand pounds, and obtained the money yesterday in the hope that you could earn it."

" Earn it! It's a large sum !"

" An *enormous* sum,—the greatest I have ever paid for an individual service."

" I suppose you want something impossible."

" To a woman so beautiful and talented as Mrs. Bradley Dashton, nothing should be impossible."

The woman sat watching him. She knew her man, and the thought that the money was within her reach was so sweet that she postponed as far as possible the stating of the condition which she felt sure must shatter her hopes.

" Well," she said, at last, " what do you want me to do ?"

Schouloff became suddenly very grave.

" Emily Dashton," he said, " I know no Englishwoman who can work with your promptitude and finesse. You have often served me in what may be called police-cases : I have never employed you in political intrigue. I am going to give you a commission higher than any you have executed hitherto."

" Why don't you give it to Bella-Demonia?" asked she, suspiciously.

" Because the Baroness Altdorff is at this moment in Turkey,—for her health."

" Well, what is it? I'll do your commission,—whatever it is," concluded she, desperately.

" Good ! If you *can*, I know you will ; but it is something higher than the stealing of a letter or the extortion of a confession. Listen ! You are bidden to a dinner at Lord Arlingford's to-night."

" Yes."

" To meet Captain Aubyn Goddard."

" Yes."

" He starts by the night-express from Charing Cross by Dover, for Vienna, *en route* for Constantinople, with governmental despatches of the highest importance."

" Yes, yes. Go on."

"He must not go."

"WHAT?"

"He must be detained."

"And who is to detain him?" asked the woman, with an expressive shrug of the shoulders.

"You."

"I!"

"Exactly."

"Prince Schouloff, do you realize what you have asked?"

"Do you realize that you have asked for *ten thousand pounds?*"

"Do you know Aubyn Goddard?"

"By reputation,—well."

"And how do you suppose he is to be prevented from doing his duty?"

"I have not the vaguest idea. If I had, I should save ten thousand pounds."

For a full minute the two sat looking at each other, the man deadly calm, the woman evidently profoundly agitated. At last she spoke.

"If this is the price of the money, I had better abandon all hope of it. The thing is grotesquely impossible. You know, as well as I do, that from the moment he leaves Arlingford's till he enters the train at Calais he will be watched by armed men. How can he be stopped?"

"He cannot be stopped. Besides, I do not want him stopped,—only detained: till to-morrow morning will be sufficient. The delay of his despatches for a few hours is all that is necessary. Force is out of the question: he must not start."

"And you expect me to prevent him,—to keep him in London?"

"You knew him in India, did you not?"

"Yes," answered the woman, with a flush, "but that was all over years ago. I have no more power over him than—than you have."

"Well," said Schouloff, looking at his watch, "I must go. It is four o'clock. Between this and midnight a woman like you might wreck an empire. Think it over: do not throw down your cards before you have played a single one. I dine at the Duke's to-night: at ten I shall drop in at the Arlingfords'. At eleven you will put your scheme, whatever it may be, into operation. At twelve the mail will go without the Queen's Messenger,—I hope. And at one I shall have the honor of waiting upon you with ten thousand pounds,—I hope. Now, *au plaisir* and *à bientôt.*"

And before Mrs. Dashton could say another word he had left the room. As the rattle of his cab-wheels died away in the distance, Mrs. Dashton dropped into her chair, and lay there motionless, her eyes fastened on the wall before her.

CHAPTER III.

CAPTAIN AUBYN GODDARD.

It was nine o'clock.

In the drawing-room of Arlingford House, Piccadilly, Mrs. Bradley Dashton sat in a low arm-chair before the fire in much the same attitude as we left her at her own house in Mayfair. The lights were turned low, but the butler was making a tour of the room, turning them up one by one.

" Dinner is not over yet, Cookson ?" remarked she.

" Not yet, ma'am. Dinner was late."

" When Major Carteret arrives, show him in here."

" Yes, ma'am."

To judge by the expression on Mrs. Bradley Dashton's face, her plans had not undergone any simplification since the afternoon, and she had evidently arrived at that point at which there is nothing to be done save to await developments from external sources. It was therefore with a sigh of relief and anticipation that she rose and moved towards the door as Cookson a few moments later drew aside the portières, announcing,—

" Major Carteret."

" How late you are !" she exclaimed, hurriedly. " I began to be afraid that you wouldn't get here before dinner was over——"

" What ! doubt *me ?* And after so much devotion to the cause,— after foregoing a charming dinner here and rushing through my solitary one at the Club on purpose to serve you ? Really, my dear child——"

" You're too civil to have any good news," interrupted she. " Keep your society manner for Lady Arlingford. You're only truthful when you're disagreeable. Be disagreeable now ; for I want the truth. Have you been able to raise the money ?"

" I regret to say that it was impossible."

" Well, what's to be done ?"

" I don't know. There's only Schouloff left. I saw him this afternoon, and he hinted that you could be of service to him. I suppose you've seen him ?"

" Yes, I've seen him."

" And can he help us ?"

" Yes, if——"

" If ! Good God ! listen to her ! As though there could be any 'if' ! Of course you'll do what he wants. What is it ?"

" Captain Goddard leaves to-night for Vienna with despatches——"

" Well, what has it to do with *him ?*"

" Schouloff wants him detained. That's all."

"*Oh !*"

The tone of Major Carteret's exclamation spoke volumes.

" I'm getting bored with this Goddard," said he, after a pause.

"Of course I regret that," said she, " but he's an old sweetheart of Alice Arlingford's, I think. That should make him interesting to you."

"Indeed! Why?"

"Because you have been laboring under the delusion that you might, by the employment of much strategy, induce Lady Arlingford to care for you or compromise herself. You have not succeeded, nor are you likely to succeed. You are not her 'form,' even did she intend to be so charming as to give her husband cause for alarm,—which does not, I grieve to say, seem likely. You forced your *entrée* here by lending Jack Arlingford money. Well, you are here. What advantage have you gained?"

"You are delightfully frank,—I might almost say rude. Why?"

"Because you're no use to me: so why should I be civil?"

"An admirable reason; but you might reflect——"

At this juncture Cookson the butler entered, and put an end to the colloquy by saying to Carteret,—

"His lordship desires to know if you will join them in the dining-room."

"Oh! very well," replied Carteret. "Yes." And he went.

"Who's here, Cookson?" said Mrs. Dashton when he had gone.

"Mr. Cincinnatus Q. Briggs, an American gentleman, ma'am, Master—erghem!—Mr. Charles Middleton, and Miss Middleton."

"Is that all? What made dinner late?" asked Mrs. Dashton, in quick alarm.

"They were waiting for a gentleman who sent a note at the last moment, ma'am."

"Do you know who it was?"

"I think it was——"

"Captain Goddard."

A footman made the announcement, cutting his superior short as Captain Goddard entered the room. Mrs. Dashton had resumed her seat before the fire, and the new-comer did not notice her.

"Not quite finished dinner yet, sir," said the butler. "Would you like to go into the dining-room?"

"Thanks, no. I'll wait here."

"And I'll keep you company!"

The words were spoken by Mrs. Dashton, who turned as she spoke and held out her hand. Seeing her, Goddard uttered an exclamation of surprise.

"Hullo, Dashey!" he cried. "How are you, old lady? How stunning you look! Egad! and deadly respectable, too,—for you."

"Hold your tongue. We're not in India now; and please remember it's something like seven or eight years since we met there."

"But——"

"Don't! Don't look at me and say it's impossible to remember seven or eight years. I'll take all your compliments for granted,—and I'll take a little discretion and prudence at the same time, *if* you please. Do you understand me, *Captain* Goddard?"

"Perfectly, *Mrs.* Dashton," replied he, gravely. There was a moment's pause, and then he added, with a quick intonation of suddenly-aroused suspicion in his voice,—

"What are you doing here?"

"In England?" queried she, meeting his tone with one of subdued defiance.

"No: in this house."

"Oh! on a visit."

"Whose invitation?"

"Whose business?"

"That depends."

"On what?"

"On you."

"Not on you?"

"That also depends."

The little colloquy was made with laconic rapidity. As silence reigned again, Mrs. Dashton eyed her opponent keenly, as if measuring their respective strengths. Finally, seeming to satisfy herself of her own inferiority, she resumed, in an altered tone,—

"Well, what do you want to know?"

"How you got into this house."

"By Lord Arlingford's invitation."

"So I thought!"

The woman bit her lip.

"Well, next?" she asked, containing herself with an effort.

"How long have you known Lady Arlingford?" was Goddard's next question.

"Since I arrived in England from Nice."

"So I supposed! How long is that?"

"About two months."

"How do you like her?"

"I don't know. I haven't thought."

"How does she like you?"

"I don't know. I haven't cared. How does she like *you?*"

"Well, I hope."

"Good! I'm glad to find some one she *does* care for."

"You don't like Lady Arlingford as well as her husband, do you?"

Mrs. Dashton rose with an impatient gesture.

"I'm getting a little tired of your questions," she said, petulantly. "Tell me plainly, is it 'Pax' between us?"

"Yes, if you behave yourself. Now look here, Dashey," he continued, frankly, "it's a rough thing to hurt a woman's feelings, and I hate to be hard on you, but Lady Arlingford is my cousin, and a dear friend into the bargain, and—and—well, hang it! you've no right here in the same house with her, and if you give me cause I shall be compelled to drop her a hint, and then most likely she'll——"

"Do as her husband bids her,—as all dutiful and obedient wives should!"

"Oh!" The intonation which Goddard threw into the ejaculation was unmistakable.

"*Exactly,*" said Mrs. Dashton, as if in reply. "It *is* 'Pax,' isn't it? Let us forget, forgive, and shake hands over it. I'm not going to stay long: I go abroad in less than a month: so you needn't be alarmed on Lady Arlingford's account. I must have a pleasant life, if I die for it, and if Lady Arlingford won't ask me to her house,—why, Lord Arlingford must,—that's all. I'm very little in England, but to keep my Continental friends going I must have a good house in London at my back."

"Do your Continental friends care much?"

"Of course they do,—Prince Schouloff, for instance, who entertains so charmingly, whose yacht, opera-boxes, villas everywhere, are always at my disposal. He sees me here; he likes to come to Lord Arlingford's informal little gatherings after his stately dinners and ceremonials. For Arlingford's little parties are not particularly ceremonious, are they?"

"Well,—erghem!—you're here, aren't you, old lady? so you ought to know."

He spoke lightly, but in his heart he was thinking, "Poor Alice! I wonder how I can help her." What Mrs. Dashton would have answered remains uninvented; for at that moment a rattle of the rings of the portières announced the arrival from the dining-room of Lady Arlingford and Miss Kitty Middleton.

The Countess of Arlingford, rapidly taking in the pair that rose as she entered, bowed icily as she greeted Mrs. Bradley Dashton, who returned her bow with something of defiance in the gesture of her head. The enmity of the two women was obvious to the merest observer. Turning to Goddard, however, her manner entirely changed.

"Ah, Aubyn!" she exclaimed, "I am so glad to see you! What a long while it seems since you went away! You remember Kitty, of course, and—Mrs. Bradley Dashton—Captain——"

"Captain Goddard and I have met before," said Mrs. Dashton, with a smile, "and we have just been re-cementing our friendship."

Goddard looked for a moment at the gold-headed Kitty, who stood staring at him, and then said,—

"Kitty, kiss your old pal at once!"

"Let me see," mused Kitty: "what is it the Yankee says? Oh, yes! Why, cert'nly." And with much deliberation Miss Middleton proceeded to kiss the handsome Queen's Messenger.

"Kitty," said Lady Arlingford, "do be more careful—before strangers."

"Oh," replied the girl, turning saucily with her arms still round Goddard's neck, "Mrs. Dashton won't be scared at a kiss—more or less," she added in Goddard's ear.

"So you're as wild as ever?" said the latter, who was suffering from mingled amusement and embarrassment.

"Worse a great deal," put in Lady Arlingford. "If you could have heard her at dinner——"

"Well," explained Kitty, "you wanted some one to wake you up. *You* looked like a block of marble, and you ought to be very much obliged to me for being so disreputable a person. What do you suppose I asked the Yankee, Aubyn?"

"Something more awful than usual, or you would not be so much amused. Go on: I'm ready to be shocked."

"I put on my most serious face and asked what he did when he found a more than usually high mantel-piece. He looked puzzled, and waited for an explanation: so I explained by asking if, under the circumstances, he stood on his head, so as to get his feet up, in the national attitude."

"What did he do?"

"Sold me dead. Instead of being a bit amazed or amused, he said, 'Is that out of *Punch?'*"

"Poor Kitty! how crushing!"

"Never mind. I shall survive the blow, and come up smiling for the second round. I'll get Mrs. Dashton to tell me about Prince Schouloff's adventures and crimes. I'm always so interested in any one with a Russian name,—sort of blood-curdling, isn't it? You'll tell me of the beautiful murders he's committed, won't you, Mrs. Dashton? It'll cheer me up."

"If the prince heard you," said Lady Arlingford, with a smile, "you would probably be sent to Siberia for life."

"Who is your Russian curiosity you're so keen about?" asked Goddard.

"Prince Schouloff, the Russian plenipotentiary. You know him, surely?"

"I know *of* him. An unprincipled scoundrel, from all accounts,—utterly unscrupulous,—a relentless, indomitable autocrat; in short, a thoroughly typical diplomat, who bears the reputation of uninterrupted success in his career by never having fallen a victim to the tender passion. There's a hearsay description for you."

"In that case," said Mrs. Dashton, "his days of success are numbered *now.*"

"And who is the conqueror?"

"Why, Bella-Demonia."

"And who's Bella-Demonia?" pursued Goddard.

"Oh, come on, Mrs. Dashton," broke in Kitty. "You can tell him about Bella-Demonia presently."

"You should not bore Mrs. Dashton, Kitty," said Lady Arlingford.

"Don't mind her, Mrs. Dashton," said the young woman, drawing her victim towards the billiard-room, that was separated from the drawing-room by heavy curtains. "You got to where the two spies crept out from the window-curtains, their daggers gleaming!—EEEH!"

Kitty Middleton's sentence closed with a scream. She had run into Cookson, who at that moment entered through the curtains with coffee. Recovering herself, however, she took her cup and disappeared with Mrs. Dashton.

Left alone with Goddard, Lady Arlingford seated herself by his side, saying, as she did so,—

"How long it seems since you went to India! And by what a strange collection of accidents it is that we have never met since!"

"Do you remember the day I left?" said he, in reply. "We were dreadful spoons, weren't we? Ah, I little thought then that I should come back to find you had forgotten your first sweetheart!"

"How do you know——"

"That I was your first? Why, you were only three years old when we met."

"Well, how do you know I have forgotten? But, seriously, you were in hopes of getting into active service. I heard General Saville say something of your getting a command. Is that true?"

"Partly. I expect to get an appointment that may lead to a command. General Saville's awfully fond of me,—dear old chap! He'd do anything for me, and he has great influence at head-quarters."

"Of course your knowledge of Eastern languages will help your promotion."

"Well, yes, to a certain extent. I must say that I look forward to active service as my greatest luck. I can say it to you, Alice: I feel that if the chance comes I can make a career, and my chance has come, I think. The mission on which I start to-night is of the greatest importance. Vital issues depend on the prompt delivery of my despatches: the loss of an hour might prove fatal to their effect. I am the more anxious to carry through to-night's job satisfactorily, as it will be my last service before retiring."

"But, in spite of all that, I shall hate to see you leave for Afghanistan."

"Ah, but you don't know how tired I am of being a toy soldier. I'm only a sort of postman, after all!"

"Nice thing for a Queen's Messenger to say!"

"Well, denuded of the swagger, it's much the same. I carry despatches; so does the postman. He works harder and gets worse paid, —that's all. There has been one thing about it lately, however,—an adventure that interested me immensely, and I had made up my mind to see the end of it, but I shall probably be prevented by this very stroke of good luck. And I'm just disappointed. Human nature, you know——"

"An adventure? Tell me about it."

"I will. This last August, waiting in Vienna for despatches, I went to a masquerade, and, after having been thoroughly bored by the usual round of stupidity, was just leaving, when a woman who I had noticed was being followed and annoyed by a man put herself under my escort to regain her carriage unmolested. The voice was unmistakably gentle: no one, even in that questionable place, could have presumed to be impertinent to her. You felt at once that she feared no insult: even in asking a service she had the air of conferring a favor. The charm of this confidence in herself and in me was so profound that I forgot everything else and could only speculate on the mystery. She hurried me forward till we reached a side-door and found ourselves in a lonely street, apparently far from the general entrance. Here a brougham was waiting. She jumped in. Aghast at the thought that the adventure was to end there and then, I begged to be allowed to see her again. In reply she made me promise to ask no questions of or about her, and then, giving me an invitation to breakfast the following day, said, 'Good-night, and many thanks, Captain Aubyn Goddard!'"

"She knew you! Who was she?"

"To this moment I have not the vaguest idea, beyond that she is called the Baroness Altdorff. By the time I had read her name and address on the card she had given me, her brougham was out of sight."

"You take away my breath. It is fascinating; but I suppose I need ask no more?"

"You are mistaken. Equivocal as the adventure appears in the beginning, to the end I can tell you every detail."

"Did you go to breakfast? But of course you did. What a question!"

"The address was in the suburbs. I found a little house hidden in a garden that at first appeared deserted, but at the appointed time I was admitted at once. A simplicity and elegance that bespoke the owner pervaded this charming nest. The whole place was a dumb repudiation of the feverish adventure of the night before,—all was such rattling ' good form ;' there was that crisp, get-up-early appearance which boded more the advent of a healthy English girl in her spotless cuffs and collar than of my heroine, whose entrance put an end to my reflections. She was quite unknown to me. I will spare you all description. The confidence that had been her chief attraction the night before saved a world of awkwardness. She had a strange charm, and, intelligent and often profound as her conversation on current events was, I give you my word I entirely forgot that I had never seen her before. It seemed as though we were old friends."

"What was she like? Very beautiful?"

"I really don't know."

"What an absurd answer!"

"But I mean it. I don't know if she is what is called beautiful; I don't know if she is what I thought beautiful. I only know that that is a point one ignores in her presence. I doubt if any one could describe her after seeing her."

Lady Arlingford smiled.

"You *have* described her, by not being able to describe her," she said.

Aubyn Goddard colored.

"My dear Alice," said he, "you show me I've been making an awful fool of myself."

"Aubyn," returned the woman, earnestly, "the love of a man is not foolish, in my eyes."

He started.

"Love?" said he.

"Yes, love!" she replied.

A dead silence fell between them.

CHAPTER IV.

A GAME OF ÉCARTÉ.

IT was broken by the sound of a boyish voice exclaiming behind them,—

"Hullo, Goddard! you back again? I heard my governor say you were going to Afghanistan. Is it true? I wish I could go with you." Charlie Middleton had just entered the room.

"I hope it's true," replied Goddard, pleasantly. "I think so. Are you going into the service?"

"No. The mater always begins to cry when any one says 'soldier,' and a fellow can't make his mother cry, can he?—beastly bad form. Where's my beastly sister? She's always in the way when one doesn't want her. The other day I was talking to Mrs. Dashton, and—well, catch Kitty giving a fellow a chance!—not she. Deuced fine woman, Mrs. Dashton, ain't she? I say, has she got any *Mr.* Dashton?"

"The memory of man runneth not to the contrary," quoted Goddard, a quaint look coming into his eyes. "You take my advice, Charlie, and give Mrs. Dashton a wide berth."

"Well, I think a good many people are a good deal too hard on her. She's a woman not easily understood. Now, I *do* understand her," said Charlie, with the superiority of his seventeen years.

"Come and talk to your May Queen, Charlie," called Kitty from the door of the billiard-room at this point.

"Oh, you! vulgar beggar," ejaculated Charlie, coloring helplessly. "There's a sister for a man to have!"

"Come to its May Queen, mother's darling," reiterated Kitty, laughing herself into the room. "You didn't know Charlie was his mother's darling, did you? His mother ought to have heard him calling Mrs. Dashton the May Queen."

At this point Charlie Middleton's overtaxed forbearance became too much for him: he made a wild rush for his escaping sister which took them both out of the room.

"What a good girl that is," said Lady Arlingford, "in spite of her wild tongue! I don't know what I should do without her."

"Is it true that she's to marry Dick Saville?"

"Yes: they were made for each other; but I shall miss her sadly. She is always ready with a cheery word to dispel the very worst attack of blues. My life would be much worse without her."

"Worse?"

"I—I mean—I meant to say I don't make friends quickly: you know I am not what the French call 'expansive,' and as one gets older——"

Goddard had been watching her color come and go as she strove to retrieve her slip of the tongue, and now he interrupted her gravely.

"Alice," said he, "what does all this mean? You are not like your old self. We were boy and girl together for as long as we can remember; friendship and affection like ours do not fade with the

years that pass us by,—no, dear,—and my affection for you tells me
more than I dreaded to hear. I have kept silent long enough,—too
long, it may be. Vague rumors have reached me, which I have not
heeded, thinking that you would speak if there was aught to say.
Tell me, what is your trouble?"

"Trouble? Why, what an alarmist you are!"

"That is no answer. Look here, Alice: I am going away to-night,
possibly for months, and I must come straight to the point. We will
speak plainly. It is no use pretending not to know what the world
says of Arlingford. The world is not always—or often—right; but—
what is Mrs. Bradley Dashton doing here? why do you admit her?"

"I—my dear Aubyn, you know very little of Jack Arlingford, to
ask me such a question. He invites his own friends, and Mrs. Dashton
is one of them. Let us talk of something else."

"No, we will talk of nothing else. I want to hear something
of your life since your marriage. In all your letters you have been
strangely reticent on this subject. Lots of gossip, but not a word of
yourself. I believe I am the only man whose relationship to you gives
him a right to question your husband."

"A right! My dear boy, you are so impetuous. If I do not
complain, why should you? Why insist on pursuing an unpleasant
subject? Do you not see I am content? I made a mistake, that's all."

"That's all! When I heard of your marriage—I was in Calcutta
at the time—I wondered how your puritanical mother's consent had
been won. Everybody knew Jack Arlingford's past. It would not
have been telling tales out of school, in his case, and I wished that at
that time I could have been in London. When I came home soon
after, you seemed happy, and—and—I think I must have been a fool
not to look deeper into my old play-fellow's heart."

"And if there was no heart to search?"

"Ah! but how you are changed! You will not complain, you are
too brave, and I was wrong to ask what you desire should remain
unasked. Forgive me; I'm a blundering soldier; but remember, dear,
I'm always your friend, and if you can ever break the ice that binds
your confidence, count on me. Count on me, dear, to the last."

For an instant Lady Arlingford's lips trembled; then, breaking
down, she hid her face in her hands.

"Oh, why has God so punished me?" she murmured. "I thought
I was stronger."

"Now I have made you cry! Don't give way," said Goddard,
helplessly. "What have I said?"

"Not you,—not you," answered the woman. "I thought I was
hardened; but—if you only knew what my life has been."

"Won't you tell me? Perhaps you think things are worse than
they really are."

"*Think!* There *is* nothing worse than my life. God never con-
demned a creature to misery more deep than mine. But come! forget
what I have said. Don't be frightened; you see I am unstrung. I
am not ill, but I think it is good to unburden my heart: it is not so
hard to confide in you. But I had made up my mind never to speak

of my trouble: I have no patience with women who have but one idea of relief,—the divorce court. I would sooner die than show the world my sorrow."

"You may carry that reticence too far. I would stake my life you are not to blame."

"You might hold me blameless. You know me, have known me all my life. But can you say to the world, 'Here is a girl, brought up by a good simple mother in the simple faith of marry, love, and obey your husband,—an honest, uninteresting creed that thousands of women live up to. This girl is married to "a man of the world." She is full of belief in the holy bond; her illusions are unbroken, and her faiths supreme. One by one they snap, as all in her finds no response in him. She fades and withers. The world asks, "What is his crime?" It seeks a crime punishable by law, as if the atmosphere of his presence were not crime enough!' Oh, the curse of our false, worldly society, which demands position at *any* cost, which admits a man with *any* past, nor inquires further than his *title!* 'Her ladyship' makes up for all shortcomings. Of *this* is the world created by Fashion, but it is not the world created by God."

"Poor girl! poor girl! what can I say? How can I advise you?"

"There is no advice I *could* take,—for the child's sake. My poor little girl would be the worst sufferer. How can I brand the father without branding the child? For her sake I will endure; but it is almost beyond endurance. I have told you so much that I may as well tell you the last infamy. I missed my pearl necklace some days ago. The same evening, that woman, who was going to the theatre with us, was standing in front of that glass as I came into the room. As she saw me she hastily unclasped something from her neck. My heart stood still; I cannot tell why, but I am convinced she had my necklace!"

"You do not think she stole it!"

"Not for a moment. *He* gave it her."

"I cannot believe that any man, no matter how bad, could be so lost to shame as to offer any woman such an insult!"

In the excitement under which they both labored, neither had heard a slight movement beyond the curtains of the billiard-room. Unperceived by them, Mrs. Dashton had been about to enter the room, when the instinct of her class bade her listen. She was eagerly drinking in the whole conversation.

"I am *not* mistaken," resumed the countess. "My shame comes to me a thousand times over as I speak of it. How I have endured that woman's presence so long I do not know. Do you think because I look passionless that I do not feel, that I cannot see, the scarce-concealed sneers of the women, the open, half-proffered pity of the men around me? I have borne it all till now; but the end has come, and if my suspicion about the necklace should prove correct——"

"Yes, yes," interrupted Goddard, eagerly, "sometimes a momentary impulse may determine what has been a long and weary struggle; and should such an impulse come to you, do not hesitate to command me. There is nothing I would not sacrifice for you!"

" Boooh !"

"Goodness! how you startled me !"

The speakers were Kitty Middleton and Mrs. Dashton. The former had come running in through the billiard-room, and had seized the latter round the waist as she came.

" I'll lay an even tenner," said the girl, cheerily, as they entered together, " that Mrs. Dashton's been listening. You know the proverb ? How do you come out, Mrs. Dashton ?"

" Kitty, you're too bad !" expostulated Lady Arlingford. " I hope Mrs. Dashton will excuse you."

" Of course she will," returned Kitty. " I've got a capital story to tell her while we put our hair straight and powder our noses. It's mildly improper. Come along. The men are coming in."

And before Mrs. Dashton could say a word, she had been whisked out of the room again.

At this moment there entered from the dining-room, laughing and talking together, Lord Arlingford, Major Carteret, and Mr. Cincinnatus Q. Briggs.

" Ah, Goddard ! glad to see you again," said his lordship, shaking Goddard by the hand. " Sorry you were detained. Major Carteret, Captain Goddard—Mr. Briggs. Mr. Briggs will be glad to ask you some questions about Berlin that I couldn't answer. I know you can. He is doing Europe; and I tell him no one is better able than you to give him the information he seeks."

" Only too happy," replied Goddard, bowing. " I fancy I knew a brother of yours, Mr. Briggs. He was painting at Leipsic—Horace I think his name was. Am I right ?"

" Perfectly," replied Briggs. " He often spoke of you, and he gave me a letter of introduction which your absence from London has prevented my using."

" I need not say, command me. I am, unfortunately, obliged to leave town to-night, on urgent business; but I hope to be back in about a fortnight. Come and have a chat then and tell me what I can do."

" Thank you. I shall come with pleasure."

Mr. Cincinnatus Q. Briggs was a most disappointing American, —that is, from the English point of view of Kitty Middleton. His clear-cut face was innocent of goatee, his clothes, though of Gothamite origin, fitted him with a precision worthy of Saville Row or Conduit Street, his full deep voice was guiltless of the least suspicion of twang, he neither hazarded " guesses" on subjects under discussion nor spent his time in vain " calculations" concerning the affairs of life. He never " reckoned," nor did he " enthuse." He ate with a fork in the regulation manner, and, whilst justly proud of the Yellowstone Park and the Yosemite Valley, did not dismiss Vesuvius with the reflection that his country boasted a waterfall that could extinguish it in two minutes. In fact, instead of being an American gentleman, he was a gentlemanly American; and Kitty Middleton, who watched to see him put his feet on the table and wave a handkerchief embroidered with the stars and stripes, was disappointed and annoyed.

As he turned to Lady Arlingford, the master of the house remarked to Goddard,—

"You go to-night, I understand? Things seem pretty lively at the Foreign Office. 'What's to be the end of it all?' is the only question one hears nowadays, and no one seems able to answer it. By the way," continued he, lowering his voice, "Mrs. Dashton tells me you knew her in India."

"Yes: most of our fellows can claim that—honor. I scarcely expected to meet her here,—or in the same house as any man's *wife.*"

The words were spoken with bitter emphasis, and the speaker turned on his heel, to be immediately tackled by Charlie Middleton, who had entered with the men. Arlingford looked after him and muttered between his teeth,—

"You shall pay for that, you puppy!"

Mrs. Dashton, entering the room at that moment, caught his expression, and came up to him with a mischievous smile on her face.

"Tt-tt-tt!" said she. "Has he been scolded by his wife's friend, —naughty boy? Goddard's affection for Alice is really quite touching, isn't it?"

"Don't play the fool!" was the courteous rejoinder. "What did Schouloff say? Can he let us have the money?"

"Ye-es."

"What does he want for it?"

"More than I can do."

"Nonsense! you must do anything he says. I *must* have it."

"He wants Goddard detained to-night. He must be delayed at any cost. This is the price of the loan."

"Oh!"

"Exactly. What do you think about it?"

"How *can* he be detained?"

"I think I know a way, if you will consent."

"If! when you know I must have the ten thousand by Monday or be posted!"

"Very well. Let me wear the pearl necklace to-night. I brought it with me."

"The necklace! Why—how——?"

"Ask no questions. Yes or no?"

"No,—not that."

"All right: manage for yourself."

"Hang it, Emily! don't be angry with me."

"Then don't be a fool!"

"I'll—I'll decide in ten minutes." And Arlingford turned and walked into the billiard-room.

Left alone, Mrs. Dashton's face was crossed by a look of triumph.

"So, my lady," said she to herself, "pure and passionless as you pretend to be, you can feel! So can I, when I am unwelcome. You have sneered at me long enough. What did you say? If your suspicions about the necklace were true, your patience would not last. We shall see! and you, Captain Goddard, will have an opportunity of making your sacrifice for friendship."

Then she joined the group at the fireplace.

"That's right; go on,—pitch into me," Kitty was saying from her position on the floor by Lady Arlingford's side, "but all my escapades are knocked into fits by Bella-Demonia's. Mrs. Dashton has been telling me about her. Who knows her?"

"By reputation, everybody," said Major Carteret.

"Everybody but the Wild Westerner," put in Briggs; and then, as they looked at him for an explanation,—it being prior to Buffalo Bill's visit to London,—he went on: "Miss Middleton told me I should have appeared in my native costume,—that is to say, beads, feathers, wampum, and a tomahawk,—and wanted to know if we hunted buffaloes on Broadway and Wall Street. I revenged myself by treating her to the dear old stand-by about Bears being the indigenous animals of those jungles. She didn't know what I meant."

"Didn't I!" said Kitty, indignantly. "But I knew you were making an old stock joke, or I'd have said I was Irish, just to get in the Bull."

"Mr. Briggs," said Lady Arlingford, as the American was about to reply, "as an old friend of Kitty's let me tell you it is hopeless trying to 'sit on' her. She will not be sat upon."

"I am patient," replied Briggs. "But may I not know more of Miss Middleton's latest shock, Bella-Demonia?"

"I did not suppose," said Carteret, "that there was a man who had not heard of her. To tell all her adventures would fill another 'Arabian Nights.' Strange that her name should be unknown to you! No woman is more talked about, and personally less known: she is more abused and praised than any living creature; I never heard her name spoken in any society that her defenders were not as earnest as her abusers. One thing is sure enough, she must be a very remarkably intelligent woman, for she certainly puzzles both friends and enemies alike."

"Did you never meet her?" asked Briggs.

"No. I believe she has never been known to receive any one on simply social grounds. Politics are her sphere, and it is remarkable that she never makes a mistake. A man may be admitted to her circle who has apparently no more value as a politician than I have as a milliner, but it always turns out that he was the one man who was vitally necessary to this or that plot. Volumes could be filled with stories about her."

"But the stories told about her are generally untrue," put in Mrs. Dashton. "*I* know her well. She is one of the most generous creatures imaginable. If any one in distress wants *anything*, off they go to Bella-Demonia."

As she said this, Arlingford entered the room unperceived, accompanied by Prince Schouloff, and remained in conversation with him in the background. The prince's tall figure was clad in evening dress, the black-and-red ribbon of St. Vladimir across his waistcoat, and the jewel of the order hanging below his cravat.

"She must be rich, to live as she does," resumed Briggs.

"Fabulously," replied Mrs. Dashton. "I must confess, I envy her. A woman with unlimited money and brains is rare enough to excite

that feeling in any one. But we are boring Lady Arlingford horribl:
You do not care to hear of interesting people, do you, Lady Arlin;
ford?"

"When they are not reputable,—no," replied her ladyship, quietl:
"I am sorry to say I cannot so far live up to the times as to adm
those people to be interesting."

"What do *you* say, Captain Goddard?" said Mrs. Dashton. "Dor
you think Bella-Demonia interesting?"

"Yes, and no," replied he. "My principal feeling is one of pity,-
of sorrow. I cannot forget that she is a woman, and a woman wl
fights against the world must at best be the loser."

"The sentiment I should expect to find expressed by so brave
soldier as Captain Goddard," said Prince Schouloff, "whom," he co
tinued, as Lady Arlingford presented them, "I have long hoped
meet, and am charmed to know."

The two men shook hands.

"May I add to your information?" pursued the prince. "Mu
has been said, and much has been written, of Bella-Demonia. She
relentless in her hate as she is gentle in her love. Revenge is h
life,—revenge for her wrongs. Once hear her speak of them, and t:
name she is known by suits her to perfection."

"But what is her real name?" asked Briggs.

"No one knows," replied Carteret.

"Or no one who knows tells," put in Mrs. Dashton.

"Bella-Demonia never lets any one know what she wishes to ɪ
main unknown," concluded Prince Schouloff; then, turning to Goddard, he added, "I have just come from the Duke's, where I heard
of your probable promotion,—from General Saville. Let me congratulate you."

"Thanks."

"Will you call on me to-morrow?"

"Very sorry I can't. I leave London to-night."

"Well, it is a pleasure deferred. A soldier is always the slave of
his duty. If I were a woman I would never have a soldier lover. I
am sorry we cannot improve our acquaintance now: however, call on
me when you return,—or in Berlin. I shall be there in a week, and
I will present you to Bella-Demonia."

Goddard bowed and rejoined the others. The prince looked after
him.

"Perhaps you will not go," said he to himself; and, taking a tele-
gram from his pocket, he read, "'The despatches carried by Captain
Goddard contain ultimatum; their detention imperative. Explanation
and further instructions by messenger.' Well, well, life is uncertain:
the young man thinks he will start to-night on his mission,—*I* think
he will not. Which of us is right, I wonder?" And he seated himself by a bookcase and began idly turning over the leaves of an album.

"I say, Mrs. Dashton," cried Charlie Middleton to that lady, who
was conversing with Lord Arlingford, "you promised to play me a
game of billiards. Come now, while they're not looking, and we'll
study the game."

"Will you be very good if I do?"

"Awfully!" replied the boy, and started for the billiard-room.

"Will you spare me to this bad child?" said she to Arlingford, as she rose.

"I wish I were the bad child!" returned he, and as he spoke he took the hand that hung by her side and pressed it. The action was not lost upon Lady Arlingford, who happened to be looking in their direction, and Goddard, noticing her change of color, followed the direction of her eyes and grasped the situation.

Lord Arlingford walked over to Prince Schouloff.

"I am afraid, prince," said he, "that you find it dull."

"Oh, no," replied Schouloff, looking him straight in the eyes. "We shall all be much amused, I hope, presently. When one has an object to serve, all things are amusing. Er—Captain Goddard must soon go. So will I." And he returned to the study of the album.

"What did Emily mean, I wonder?" reflected Arlingford, recalled to actualities by the prince's words and manner. "Can it be that if she wears the necklace Goddard will resent the affront and delay his departure? Ah!"—and a new light broke in upon him,—"she's right, as usual. We shall see; we shall see."

"It seems as though when you go," Lady Arlingford was saying to Goddard, "I shall be at the mercy of that creature."

"Cheer up, little woman," he answered. "Don't give way. Pretend you don't care: it's the worst punishment you could inflict."

"Come and see a catastrophe," broke in Kitty. "I'm going to spoil sport. I want to show you how Mrs. Dashton teaches Charlie billiards. Nice game, billiards. Listen! not a sound. Follow me."

She started towards the billiard-room, accompanied by Carteret and Briggs, and Lady Arlingford pursued her to prevent the accomplishment of her vile purpose. Goddard was following, when Arlingford, who had been watching for the opportunity, stopped him.

"Look here, Goddard," said he, "you are an old friend of Alice's. I wish you'd advise her to be more civil to Mrs. Dashton."

"You must do your own dirty work," replied Goddard, hotly; "and, by God, sir, *that's* not the advice I would give your wife, even if I had less regard for her than I have! You ought to send that woman away."

"Really, Goddard," answered Arlingford, haughtily, "upon my word I don't understand you."

"Yes, you do! and you make my position doubly difficult by evading the question."

"By what right do you *dare* question my actions?"

"By the rights of blood and friendship!"

"For my wife! I fail to recognize the right. Now look here: I've been patient long enough. I'm sorry you're in love with my wife——"

"In love! Stop——"

"But she *is* my wife," continued Arlingford, imperturbably, "and I forbid you to see her any more. Do you hear?"

"You hound!" cried Goddard, "if I didn't respect her feelings, I'd thrash you in your own house." Then, as the others, attracted by his tone, re-entered from the billiard-room, he added, "For her sake, no scene now; but later on you and I will settle."

"What is the matter?" said Lady Arlingford, anxiously, as she came between them. "You are quarrelling!"

"No, no," said Goddard; "only arguing."

"A trifle warmly, perhaps," added Arlingford. "We were disputing a point at écarté. We will settle it now, if you like, Goddard. I'll bet you a hundred pounds I'm right."

"So be it: we shall see."

Kitty Middleton, who saw that something was amiss, busied herself with Charlie getting the card-table ready, whilst Arlingford rapidly sorted out the unnecessary cards from the pack and threw them on a side-table. Throughout the above scene Prince Schouloff had sat apparently absorbed in the album he had taken up. Arlingford and Goddard seated themselves at the table and began to play. Carteret and Briggs were standing in a bow-window, discussing American finance, Lady Arlingford was alone by the fire, and Kitty sat at the piano close beside her, running her fingers lightly over the keys.

As the game began, Mrs. Dashton strolled in from the billiard-room. As she did so, the prince looked at his watch. It was eleven. In a quarter of an hour Goddard must be gone. Mrs. Dashton came to Arlingford's side, and whispered,—

"Well? The prince grows impatient. Am I to aid you?"

"Wear the necklace!" said he, desperately.

"The despatches will be detained: you will get the money," she whispered, adding to herself as she left the room, "Goddard will be ruined, and 'Dashey' will have scored one!"

As she went out, Prince Schouloff strolled over to Lady Arlingford's side.

"Lady Arlingford," said he, "I do not see you much in society now, and you look pale. I hope you are not suffering? You should go abroad for a time. Lord Arlingford must bring you to Nice, and you, Miss Middleton, must come also."

"Kitty will not be Miss Middleton for long, prince," answered Lady Arlingford for her.

"Then I shall look forward to welcoming Mr. and Mrs. Saville wherever I may be," answered Schouloff, with a bow to Kitty.

At this moment Mrs. Dashton entered the room, wearing a row of magnificent pearls round her neck. Lady Arlingford, catching sight of them, started violently, and Prince Schouloff said, in the quiet careful tone that alone betrayed the fact that he was a foreigner,—

"What beautiful pearls you have, Mrs. Dashton! Excuse me, but I had not noticed them before."

"Yes," answered she, carelessly, "they *are* pretty. A present."

Goddard turned his head, and his eyes fell on the necklace. Lady Arlingford was steadying herself with difficulty against her chair.

"You cowardly blackguard!" he hissed across the table at Arlingford.

" You are my wife's champion, it would seem," sneered he. " Defend her !"

" Come and see the game, prince," said Mrs. Dashton, moving over to the card-table, where she was joined by Mr. Briggs and Major Carteret. Meanwhile, Lady Arlingford had crossed to the table where the useless cards had been thrown down, and, taking up one of them,—a two of clubs,—wrote on it hurriedly in pencil, " *I will not stay another hour in this house. I go with you.*"

Mrs. Dashton had watched her closely.

" Much on the game ?" asked she, carelessly.

" For so much excitement," said the prince, " there should be at least ten thousand pounds !"

Lady Arlingford came over to Goddard's side. There she dropped her handkerchief, and as she stooped to pick it up slipped the card on which she had written into Goddard's lap. He took it stealthily, unconscious that Mrs. Dashton had followed every movement.

Suddenly the latter stooped and whispered in Arlingford's ear.

" What is that you have hidden ?" cried he to Goddard.

" I—I do not understand," stammered Goddard.

" You have a card there, and I demand that it be shown !"

" I cannot show it."

" I did not suppose you could," sneered Arlingford, slipping a card from his hand unobserved into that of Mrs. Dashton, and flinging the rest on the table. " You see I do not hold the *king.*"

" What do you mean ?" cried Goddard, growing deathly pale.

" I mean that I do not play cards with a man who cheats !" howled Arlingford.

Goddard started to his feet.

" My God !" he exclaimed, pressing his hands to his head. As he rose, an elderly military-looking man had entered the room. It was General Saville.

" Well, how are you all ?" he exclaimed, comprehensively. " Aubyn, I bring you good news, my boy. To-night's mission will be your last. I have gained my point with the Duke, and he has confirmed your staff-appointment." Then, observing for the first time the dead silence and the dismayed faces round him, he continued,—

" What is the matter ? Why don't you speak, some of you ?"

" I repeat," said Arlingford, with deadly distinctness, "your methods are not such as to permit gentlemen to play cards with you, and I must desire that you leave this house at once."

" Arlingford," cried General Saville, " how dare you ! You must be mad. I demand an explanation."

" Captain Goddard holds a card that was not dealt to him, which he refuses to show, and which I assert is the king of clubs."

" Good heavens ! Deny it, Aubyn : tell him he lies !"

" Mrs. Dashton and Prince Schouloff also saw him take the card from his lap," continued Arlingford, calmly.

" Answer !" thundered the general, growing purple.

" It is a lie," said Goddard, quietly.

" Then show the card," said Arlingford.

"Yes, show the card," cried the general.

"I cannot."

A dead silence fell in the room. It was broken by the sound of a fall. Unobserved, during the above scene Lady Arlingford had been struggling to speak. An iron grip seemed to be upon her throat, and she struggled in vain. As Goddard spoke, she fell senseless to the floor.

"Captain Goddard," said General Saville, stiffly, "it will be obvious to you that there is only one course for you to pursue. I will save you the trouble of resigning your commission, and your diplomatic post is vacant. You will take your name from your Club lists to-morrow, and—God! boy," concluded the old gentleman, all but breaking down, "I'd sooner you'd been a murderer than a blackleg."

General Saville turned, and, seeing Schouloff, went towards him. Goddard looked round him for a moment, and, seeing even Kitty's face averted as she bent over Lady Arlingford, exclaimed,—

"Ruined! God help me!"

And he rushed from the room.

*　　　*　　　*　　　*　　　*　　　*　　　*　　　*

An hour later, in the little Mayfair drawing-room Prince Schouloff paid over to Mrs. Bradley Dashton ten thousand pounds in Bank-of-England notes.

Not a word was said on either side.

BOOK III.

CHAPTER I.

IN A POLITICAL OBSERVATORY.

THE political crisis which opened the year 1876 with the "Andrassy Note" closed it with the Conference at Constantinople of January, 1877. By the middle of that month the Cabinets of Europe had realized the fact that the Conference had been met by a rejection of its proposals on the part of the Sublime Porte, and at the end of March the Six Powers forwarded to the Sultan their ultimatum in the form of a Protocol. Turkey, however, pursued her time-honored policy of masterly inactivity, and on the 24th of April Europe was startled by the news that Russia had declared war against the Sultan in defence of the Christian populations of the Balkan Peninsula, had crossed the Pruth into Roumania, which had promptly declared itself on the side of the Muscovite, and had entered Asia Minor at Batoum, Kars, and Bayazid.

The only explanation vouchsafed to Europe was contained in the circular note of Prince Gortschakoff, and the Powers, after entering their formal protest, assumed a position of armed neutrality.

The campaign opened, as is familiar to the student of modern history, with a series of Russian successes both in Europe and Asia. General Gourko crossed the Danube without opposition in June, and invested Tirnova on the 7th of July, preparatory to crossing the Balkans at Yeni Saghra five days later with a flying column. It was not till then that Russia saw the mistake she had made in overlooking Plevna, and turned in that direction to find it occupied and fortified by the greatest general of the Ottoman forces, Osman Pasha. On the 20th and on the 31st of July two desperate assaults of this position resulted in the total defeat of the Russian arms, and Gourko was driven back beyond the Balkans, whilst in Asia Moukhtar Pasha gained his first decisive victory at Kars.

Thus, in August, 1877, when our story reopens, the Muscovite advance had received a temporary but serious check, Todleben had been called to the investment of Plevna, and the nations looked at one another with apprehensive glances as they asked themselves and one another, " What next ?"

Meanwhile, the principal post of observation established by Russia in the Balkans was at the village of Deve-kiui, on the road from Eski Saghra to Adrianople, where, snugly established in the Villa Kristov Hisar, Prince Schouloff and the Baroness Altdorff anxiously watched the successive turns which events were taking.

A few weeks before this they had been joined by Mrs. Bradley Dashton, who since we parted from her in London had suffered a series of reverses in the prosecution of her plans. Indeed, important events and changes had taken place in the lives of most of the actors in the drama with which we are concerned, all resulting directly and indirectly from the tragedy enacted at Arlingford House on the night that saw the successful issue of the plot concocted against Captain Aubyn Goddard.

For weeks Lady Arlingford had lain unconscious between life and death. In her delirium she had raved much about that fatal evening, but her utterances had been ascribed to the state of her brain; and when she recovered from the blow and emerged into the light of reason, Goddard was to all intents and purposes lost to the world. As soon as she could be moved, Alice Arlingford had been taken to her mother's house in Berkeley Square, and here Kitty Middleton had been her only *confidante.* To her she had told the whole dismal story as soon as she was sufficiently herself to do so, and both agreed that to publish the facts now, in the absence of Goddard, would be to lay themselves open to the charge of having invented the story to clear the man whom Arlingford had—though vainly—tried to brand as his wife's lover. So they had waited on in the hope that Goddard might be heard of again, and that he might be summoned home to assist in his own exculpation from the charges brought against him by the Earl of Arlingford, Mrs. Dashton, and Major Homer Carteret.

One step, however, had been taken which the events of the evening and the episode of the necklace had rendered inevitable: this was the divorce of the Earl and Countess of Arlingford, which went by default in the absence of his lordship and upon the admissions of Mrs. Dashton. Soon after the disappearance of Goddard, Arlingford had found that the glances bestowed upon him in club-rooms, never of the warmest, had become arctic in their frigidity. He found that men refused to hear the name of Aubyn Goddard spoken by his lips, and that his efforts to deepen the cloud which rested over the ex Queen's Messenger were practically abortive. Under these circumstances, his lordship had betaken himself to the more congenial atmosphere of Nice and Monte Carlo, whither Mrs. Dashton had shortly after followed him, and, after passing six months of varied fortune at the tables, found himself in the, to him, familiar predicament of being "cleaned out." It was then that the summons of Prince Schouloff had seemed to Mrs. Dashton laden with the pleasant perfume of hope, and, obeying it, armed with passes through the Russian lines, she had joined the Prince and Bella-Demonia in their political observatory, anxious to serve the Chief of Police for the furtherance of her own plans, which seemed to have encountered a serious and abiding check.

The divorce of the Countess of Arlingford and the marriage of Kitty Middleton to Dick Saville had taken place almost simultaneously, and thus a powerful ally had joined the campaign for the rehabilitation of Aubyn Goddard.

Of Goddard himself the news had been at first scanty, then depressing, and finally overwhelming. What might have been the effect on European history had he started on that fatal night with his despatches, it is not for us to conjecture. He had reached Charing Cross five minutes too late, and had laid his despatches with his resignation on his chief's table at eight o'clock on the following morning, and they had left London with another messenger by the ten-o'clock mail. Later in the day he had had a long interview with General Saville, from which the sturdy old warrior had emerged with something very like a tear in the one eye that active service had left him, and had emphatically remarked to a Club crony,—

"Damn the boy! I love and admire him more than ever. He won't tell me anything about it, but I'll swear"—which he did with unction—"that a more honorable fellow never lived. Some day we shall get to the bottom of this miserable affair; meanwhile, we can only wait and hope for the best."

General Saville took upon himself to lay Goddard's resignations, with a statement of the circumstances, before the committees of his various Clubs, and those illustrious bodies had decided to hold his membership in abeyance, pending an inquiry and explanation.

On the following day Goddard had started for America, bound for a ranch owned by General Saville in Dakota Territory. A few months later, one of the periodical revolutions having eventuated in Central America, Goddard's soldier instinct overcame him, and he had placed himself at the head of a regiment of *filibusteros*, on the side of the existing government. In one of the decisive engagements he had performed deeds of unheard-of valor, and had been reported dead,—killed by a stray shot at the moment of victory,—and so he had gone out of this history, and his record was to all intents and purposes closed.

Things were in this condition when our story reopens at the Villa Kristov Hisar in Bulgaria, in the month of August, 1877.

Prince Schouloff sat in his study, which looked out upon the veranda of the villa, going over a bundle of despatches, and ever and anon consulting a map that lay before him. At his elbow stood his private secretary, Dmitri Keratieff, awaiting the attention of his chief.

"Well," said the prince, looking up from his map, "what have you to report?"

"Mrs. Dashton tried to open the mail-bag early this morning: she said she had enclosed a letter by mistake. I opened it for her: there was no letter of hers in the bag. Madame von Altdorff sent a despatch by her courier-secretary before daylight."

"Ah! Know you its contents?"

"No, Excellency. I am more useful alive than dead, and I never question the incoming or outgoing of Rodia Pouschkoff."

The secretary laughed as he spoke, and Schouloff nodded his head gravely but approvingly.

"Did you see him start?"

"Yes, Excellency. He took the direction of Eski Saghra."

"He has not returned?"

"Not yet."

"Anything else?"

"Mrs. Dashton bade me present her compliments and say that she desired to speak with your Excellency as soon as you should be at leisure."

"Where is she now?"

"On the terrace."

"Ask her to honor me with a visit, here and now."

The secretary retired.

"Ah, Emily Dashton," soliloquized the prince, "you are unable to control your curiosity; you are madly eager to know why I sent for you. Take care! You are an excellent servant, but you can never direct. Examine my mail-bag! how *rococo!* The method has neither novelty nor ingenuity to recommend it, and still, undaunted, you play your little, your *very* little, tricks."

And Prince Schouloff, leaning back in his chair, laughed aloud, as Mrs. Dashton appeared at the French window leading out upon the terrace.

"Alone, and amused?" said she, looking at him from the window. "Happy man!"

"Sensible people," replied Schouloff, "never depend upon any one for anything, not even for their amusement."

"As usual, your sentiment is flawless. But are you sure you are as independent as you think?"

"It has been the study of my life to be so."

"And, like most students, you have absorbed yourself so much in the study of others that you have left no time to study yourself. You leave that for fools like me."

"Do you find me interesting?"

"Er—um—ye-es. But not so original as I expected."

"Well," said Schouloff, in the altered tone of a man desirous of changing the subject, "I will try to do better. So much for your amusement. Now for your business. I understand you wished to speak to me?"

"Yes," answered Mrs. Dashton, her manner also altering. "I am not satisfied with the way things have turned out. You offered to help me, and I carried out my part of the bargain. I knew that when Lady Arlingford saw her pearls on my neck she would do something foolish that would detain Goddard. She did more; but I am no nearer the realization of my hopes. I am getting tired of scheming, and want rest."

"Why reproach me with—pardon me!—your own folly? I wished Captain Goddard detained, and was willing to pay for it. You undertook to effect the delay, and received the payment for so doing,—an enormous sum: is it not so? It is with Lord Arlingford you are not satisfied, not with me. Come, be frank; what did he promise you? You do not answer. Well, he promised that if you would help him, he would drive Lady Arlingford to claim a divorce, and would then marry you. The first he has done; the second he has not."

"How do you know this?"

"I did *not* know; but you betray your own secrets. But your ambition is a wrong one. As a woman you are charming, as a wife you would be stupid."

"Do you suppose," broke out the woman, impetuously, "that because I have led a rough life I have no feeling? You have guessed half the situation, so hear it all. I *am fond* of Jack Arlingford. I know he's a bad lot; perhaps that's why I like him: I'm not such a very good lot myself!—and good people make me angry. He cares for me, I believe, and if everything had not gone so contrary, I think he would have kept his promise; but after the divorce everything went so wrong that I was obliged to leave London. I joined him in Nice, and now he is broke there, and cannot move a step till he gets money."

Prince Schouloff smiled.

"Shall I prove to you," he said, "that he will *not* keep his word—even so far as he can—to you?"

"How? Do you mean that he does not really care for me? If I thought that——!"

"Lord Arlingford is at this moment trying to marry a rich American, a cousin of the Mr. Briggs whom we met at his house. He cares for *nothing* save gambling, and his affection for you will be regulated by the amount you subscribe to the fund. Now, let me know the amount necessary to—your happiness, and try to find out for me accurate details as to the death of Captain Goddard. I am much interested in him."

"In Goddard? Where did you lose sight of him? Let me see: where did you lose sight of him? I think I remember. After the scandal he started for Dakota, for a ranch belonging to General Saville. There the soldier got the better of him, and he joined that Central American revolution, and was reported dead. Is that right?"

"Perfectly: you are accuracy and clearness to perfection, as far as our information goes; but I should like the details. Now, I have a charming villa at Mentone, of which I should like to make a wedding-

present to the bride who can give me accurate details of Captain Goddard's death. The certificate of the marriage is not necessary to secure
the gift."

" Which means, translated——?"

" What you please! Mrs. Dashton, you are a clever woman, especially so where the finesse of a woman's nature is concerned : witness,
for instance, your instinct in Lady Arlingford's case, where you judged
exactly the moment to strike. I should value your opinion just now.
Erghem! I see a great change in Bella-Demonia. She takes no interest in anything. I have sought in vain the reason : can you help me?"

" You once said, ' Bella-Demonia never allows any one to know
what she wishes to remain unknown.' That is my answer *now*. I am
a woman of fairly strong nerve ; but ask Bella-Demonia a question
about herself?—excuse me! See," continued she, rising, and moving
to the window, " there she is on the terrace. She looks gentle enough ;
but when she chooses to freeze you, her cold stare of wonder at your
audacity would daunt a braver woman than I. But be sure that if I
can help you I will. She is coming this way. Shall I go?"

" Not yet. See if her manner helps you."

And the prince walked to the window to meet the object of his recent
conversation.

" Who, to see her sweet soft face," thought he, " would believe that
she could be so hard to conquer? Yet for close upon a year I have
fluttered like a moth in vain around the flame of her fascination,—I,
Alexis Schouloff!"

Two quickly successive reports, the boom of a distant gun, rever-
berated dully on the air, as the Baroness Altdorff stepped into the
room, giving her hand to Prince Schouloff as she did so.

" Those were the cannon of Eski Saghra, prince. It is true, then,
that the Flying Legion has arrived in the neighborhood?"

" Such are my last instructions, baroness," returned the prince,
gravely, looking at his watch.

" What a picture you made there, baroness!" put in Mrs. Dashton
at this point,—"a living embodiment of tranquil power in repose.
Dreaming pleasant things, I judge by your expression. You are a
true subject for an artist."

" You evidently have not remarked, Mrs. Dashton," interrupted
Bella-Demonia, icily, " that I do not like flattery. From a woman it
means either nothing or a great deal too much. Prince, I shall have,
I think, great news for you before the afternoon is over. Mrs. Dashton, you have not yet visited me in my own apartments : you must
come and see me there. The prince is good enough to let me have an
entire wing to myself, where no one ever comes save at my request."

" I shall look forward to coming and seeing you *chez vous*. I have
so much yet to say to you and ask you."

" You will find me a bad gossip——"

" But I will do all that, and I am positively dying for a good long
talk. This place, with all respect to Prince Schouloff, is so far from
civilization! Upon my word, it's as hard to get here as—as—as it was
for poor Goddard to get himself killed."

She said the last words after a hesitation, as if she had been searching vainly for a simile. As she concluded, Bella-Demonia turned deathly white, but controlled herself with a violent effort which did not escape the narrow observation of Schouloff.

"What a singular comparison to make!" said she, at last.

"Perhaps it was," said Mrs. Dashton, reflectively. "I don't know what brought him to my mind at that moment. Strange break, his,—a man who was apparently just reaching the zenith of his career, or, if not quite that, with every promise for the future, to ruin himself so completely!—it is inconceivable. But why should I wander on so, about a stranger to you?—but then, you see, I knew him so well."

"You knew him?" put in Bella-Demonia, eagerly; then, recovering herself once more, she added, "*What* was the name?"

"Aubyn Goddard. I'll tell you all about it some day, when I come to see you in your own rooms."

"That will be very soon," said Prince Schouloff to himself. Then he added aloud to Bella-Demonia, "You are interested, baroness?"

"Naturally! A man who ruins himself at the very moment that his prospects seemed most bright must have had the usual cause,—a woman. Hence the story must be at least amusing."

"Then you believe," said the prince, "that when a man is ruined, a woman is always the cause. Oh, fie!"

"Not at all, in the way you put it. A man may be ruined by many causes; but when he brings about his *own* ruin it is pretty safe to assume that there is a woman."

"Well," said Schouloff, "I will argue that point later."

"It must be nearly time our bold travellers arrived. I must watch from the terrace for them, in case there be any young man in the party whom I can make my own. Who are these visitors, prince?"

"They shall announce themselves to you, Mrs. Dashton."

"Well, no doubt it's some pleasant surprise you have in store for me. I won't be inquisitive. I hope I don't shock you, baroness?"

"I shocked!" returned Bella-Demonia, in an accent of ironical surprise, "I,—the byword of Europe! My right to censure or extol was stolen from me years ago."

"And *I* don't believe I ever *had* that right. Well, *au revoir*. I must go and get ready."

And Mrs. Dashton disappeared from the room with a laugh.

"Who are these visitors, prince?" said Bella-Demonia, when she had gone. "You have told me nothing."

"Because there was nothing to tell, till this morning. A Mr. Saville and his wife,—charming people: they will interest you. They want to see me,—and you,—and, arriving at the frontier two days since, applied to me for passes through the lines. They arrived at Eski Saghra last night, and are coming on this morning. The proximity of the Flying Legion has made me nervous about them."

Bella-Demonia dismissed the subject with a little shrug.

"Tell me," said she, "why did you ask that woman, Mrs. Dashton, here?"

"Because I thought she would amuse you."

" Because you wanted her to find out something for you, from me,
—from *me !*"

" If you know, why ask ?"

" To give you a chance of being honest with me. You know I
hate lies and the cowardice that begets them. Ask *me* what you want
to know. Have I ever been wanting in courage to speak ?"

" You are irritable, baroness ; yet I have been patient, and not—
not ungenerous ?"

" Forgive me, if, in the weariness I feel, I forget how much I owe
you. When I first sought you I was seeking distraction : you offered me
politics, absorbing as heart or brain could desire. I had nothing to live
for till you brought me within range of your vast world of schemes.
By degrees the fascination of your power gained on me. To see great
nations tremble or rejoice, to see life or death meted out, was the breath
of life to me. For years of feverish oblivion I have to thank you, and
I do. But I am still a woman, and my very being is weary. See the
traces !" As she spoke, she turned to the mirror over the mantel-shelf,
and leaned upon it. " If only my revenge had not been torn from me,
I would have served an eternity. If heaven had but been just to me !"

" My hope," said the Russian, gently, " has been to bring you more
than oblivion. Must that hope always be vain ? Will you never forget the cares, the sombre side of life, and remember but the glowing
sunshine which is yours by right of love ?"

He had risen and approached her as he spoke. She drew away, as
she said,—

" I thought our compact was clear. Must I remind you ? When
I accepted your service, I knew that I risked my life in a service of
danger ; that life I sold you,—if need should come, my death ; but I did
not sell you myself."

" No, that you only give. Oh, it is only ' Bella-Demonia' who is
dead to love : to find mercy, the mother of love, one must appeal to
charity. ' Carita,'—it is a sweet name, and I would call you by it."

" The name was my mother's : it is sacred to me. But come ! do
not let us speak in riddles. You know some part of my secret, you
would know more. I tell you frankly you will learn nothing through
that woman. *You* have the better chance. Question me ! I may reserve what I like, but I will not lie."

For an instant the two stood silently looking at each other, and then
the prince spoke.

" Did you care for this man Goddard ?" said he.

" With my whole soul !"

" Why did you never speak of him ?"

" That which lies near the heart is far from the lips."

" Do you know what has become of him ?"

" He is dead, if that woman spoke true. Well, so much the better
for you and for your work. You will find me the better destroyer now
that the one touch of womanhood is laid at rest forever. Direct, and I
will execute. Let me think only of wrongs and the blight they bring.
I told you I would give you news. I have news for you,—brave
news."

" Tell me, what is it?"

" The Russian arms have received a serious check. For the last month your best-laid plans of campaign have been frustrated by the unerring precision of the movements of this Flying Legion of which we hear so much and see so little: is it not so?"

" Perfectly. The latest despatches of Skobeleff are to that effect."

" Well, the chief of the Flying Legion, Beyaz Murad Bey, will be in my power to-night. What is his capture worth?"

" Murad here! It cannot be possible!"

The prince rose to his feet and commenced pacing up and down the room. The Baroness Altdorff smiled as she leaned back in her chair.

" Is that a reflection?" said she. " You are not complimentary to my powers of fascination, to say nothing of my skill as a diplomatist, —some say ' decoy.' "

" You are in earnest!" exclaimed Schouloff, coming to a full stop before her.

" Perfectly. I came to the conclusion that he must be taken out of your way. But for him, we should be in possession of the Shipka Pass. He is advancing upon Plevna. Once let him join Osman, and we shall see what the Grand Duke, Todleben, and Skobeleff can do,— such a three against such a two! I shall remove him, this terror, Beyaz Murad,—Murad Bey."

" Not easy——"

" No, not easy, but—— Well, never mind my plan of action: the result is all that you need know. Admit that I chose our location here with forethought, three months before hostilities commenced. After much delicate work, I have caused the report to reach the Chief that in consequence of your weakness—of *your* weakness!"—and she laughed a little—" I was in possession of important strategic secrets, that I had expressed great admiration of his bravery and was impressionable, —*impressionable!*—in short, that *he* might learn all I knew with a little trouble. The Flying Legion encamped last night near Eski Saghra. They are short of provisions, and knowledge of our move- ments is imperative. Well, by my arrangement he has laid a trap for me into which he will fall himself."

Prince Schouloff's eyes glowed with admiration.

" By St. Nicholas! ingenious as only Bella-Demonia could be! Perhaps this is the only one line that could have snared him. What marvellous tact! what instinct! Ah! if you are not for me, what a pity you were not born a man! You are sure he will come?"

" I await only a letter by my courier-secretary Rodia, to confirm what I say."

" Tell me, how were you inspired to such a glorious plan?"

" I wanted to earn your supreme gratitude, and, so, my freedom. I had hoped—till *she* dispelled my dream—— But never mind: since *he* is lost to me, no danger can appall me. I thought for a brief hour that I might know the joys denied me and given to others; but no! like the fabled Jew, so must *my* pilgrimage last forever. No peace! no love! naught that woman counts her right. Well, so be it!"

She covered her face with her hands as she became silent, and the interview was interrupted by the entrance of a servant bearing two cards.

"Ah, baroness," said Schouloff, as he read the names of Mr. and Mrs. Richard Saville, "our expected guests are here. They will amuse you. Mr. Saville belongs to a very good family, and finished his eccentric career by marrying an eccentric young lady,—a Miss Middleton. They call them 'The Shocks;' and we are indeed fortunate that they arrive so opportunely to enliven us."

Then, turning to the servant, he said,—

"Inform Mr. and Mrs. Saville that Prince Schouloff and the Baroness Altdorff will wait upon them immediately in the hall."

<hr>

CHAPTER II.

DICK SAVILLE.

DICK SAVILLE was an excellent specimen of the young Englishman whose personal qualities cause him to be universally dubbed "a devilish good fellow." Only son of General Saville, he had elected not to follow the profession of arms, but became Aubyn Goddard's chum at Oxford, where, with widely divergent tastes, they were as inseparable as circumstances would permit. Goddard had been a reading man and an athlete, Saville had been an athlete, but there their similarity of pursuits had ended. Notwithstanding his multifarious escapades, indulged in with the object of emblazoning the gray old university town a lively heraldic *gules*, Dick Saville was an inveterate favorite with the dons, and even in that paradise for women Dick suffered a positive embarrassment of attentions from the petticoated inhabitants of his *alma mater*. Still, the process of compelling an objectionable proctor and his bull-dog to take a midnight bath in the college fountain and proceed home in each other's clothes turned inside out is not calculated to act as an example of discipline to undergraduates, and Dick Saville returned to the bosom of his father,—who, I regret to say, roared with delight,—to spare the authorities the heart-rending task of "sending him down" covered with ignominy and unpaid bills.

At the premature close of his academic career Dick started for the Cape *en route* for Seringapatam, and, having returned home *via* India and Egypt, met Kitty Middleton at a dance at Lady Arlingford's.

In five minutes Dick realized that he had met "that other self," and historians tell us that Kitty became kissed. This duty performed, he started for Madagascar *en route* for Persia and Russia, with two flannel shirts, a tooth-brush, and a photograph of Kitty. He escaped from a horde of Koords with nothing but a pair of tattered trousers and the photograph—also tattered—of Kitty, and when he told her of his escapes observed that she grew dreadfully white and didn't laugh at or abuse him for a whole quarter of an hour. Announcing his intention of starting for New York *en route* for Japan and China, Kitty put her foot down firmly, and asked what was the maximum of luggage that *she* would be allowed to take. Dick argued that she would have to camp in very rough places, to which Kitty replied that so long as he took a thick rug and plenty of quinine she didn't care. And so at the end of the season of 1877 the *Morning Post* announced that at St. Peter's, Eaton Square, Richard Arthur Chenevix Saville, son of General Sir Richard Saville, V.C., K.C.B., had married Catherine Maude, daughter of the late Sir Cyrus Middleton, K.C.M.G. It was a " marriage," not a " wedding," and Mr. and Mrs. Saville started for Paris and Monte Carlo with one object alone in view,—to wit, the exoneration of Goddard.

So long as there was any hope of Goddard's return, Dick had agreed with Kitty and Lady Arlingford that they must wait for his assistance to this end; but now that he was dead, Dick announced his intention of taking the matter into his own hands and extorting a confession from Arlingford and Mrs. Dashton. Dick was no fool. The presence of Prince Schouloff on that fatal night, the delay of Goddard's all-important despatches, and the immediately subsequent clearance of Arlingford's most pressing liabilities had given him a clue, and when he found that nothing was to be done with Arlingford or the Dashton, he wrote for passes to Prince Schouloff, whom he personally knew, on the plea that he was anxious to pay a country-house visit in the middle of the seat of war.

Thus on this eventful afternoon Mr. and Mrs. Dick Saville found themselves in the hall of the Villa Kristov Hisar at Deve-kini, near Eski Saghra, awaiting the appearance of their host and hostess.

They had not long to wait before Schouloff appeared with Bella-Demonia.

Schouloff greeted Saville and his wife warmly.

" Let me present you," said he, " to the Baroness Altdorff, Mrs. Saville,—Mr. Saville."

" I am charmed to see you," said the baroness. " We owe a great debt to Providence for having brought you safely to us. I have ordered some tea immediately. I learnt the custom in England and Russia, and never enjoy it so much as when I am far from civilization."

" It's contrast that gives the charm to everything," replied Kitty. " Dick and I pass our lives in search of it. It was to find a contrast to the deadly respectable that made us become so disreputable. You know, we are called ' The Shocks' because we keep people in a continual state of excitement. I tell them it's good for their health. They probably consider it heroic treatment; but it's quite necessary for some complaints."

" For instance ?" queried Bella-Demonia, who was equally astonished and amused.

" Dulness and stupidity ! There is no doubt we are good for our own people, but better still for the world. Nothing amuses Dick and me so much as to devise some awful escapade,—that is, what the world is pleased to consider awful. Time after time we say, ' *This* is sure to settle us : we shall be ostracized,—kicked out.' Not a bit of good. Dick's too rich : people look upon it as a new and charming eccentricity, and that's all. But I must be boring you dreadfully. Somebody must stop me talking, or I shall go on forever."

"Don't stop!" exclaimed Bella-Demonia: "you are more than delicious. I will only interrupt you for a moment, to ask how and by what accident you are here."

"By no accident," said Dick Saville. "We came to find you, baroness, and Prince Schouloff."

"Indeed? You surprise me. What can we do for you?"

"Mrs. Saville has been telling you of some of our follies," answered Dick. "How long we should have continued to afford amusement to our friends is uncertain, because an event occurred which changed the current of my idiocy."

"Well, we won't contradict you," said Bella-Demonia, "it is so refreshing to hear you display your superior intelligence in your own way."

"Intelligence! I am trying to convince you, baroness, that I am a fool."

"I am afraid you are not succeeding very well. Still, I would not interfere with the amusement of any living creature: so I promise to assume anything you please, if you promise to continue your story."

"Oh, Dick doesn't need any inducement to talk," put in Kitty: "he runs *me* very close, and I've killed several people."

"The last time we met, Mrs. Saville," said Prince Schouloff, "I tried to make you promise to visit me at Nice. I did not expect that you would ever wander so far from the world as to make that visit here. But I am none the less indebted to you, believe me."

"You are too good, prince. It is to remind you of the time of which you speak that we have come to take you by storm."

"Since you have come so far to find us, I presume, like the Baroness Altdorff, that there is some service we may render you. For myself, pray command me; and I am sure that the baroness feels with me."

"Most assuredly," said Bella-Demonia.

"Well, then," said Dick Saville, "since I cannot convince you that I deserve to be called a fool for my pains, let me at least convince you that I can be a hard-working friend; and it is on behalf of that friendship that I have come in search of certain information and assistance. The prince has spoken of his last meeting with Mrs. Saville. On that occasion a tragedy was enacted which ruined the career of the best fellow that ever lived. I speak of Aubyn Goddard."

"Goddard!" The speaker was Bella-Demonia, who leaned forward, her eyes eagerly fixed on Dick's ugly but sympathetic face.

"Doubtless you, madame," said Kitty, "heard of the affair. I was present. It was terrible."

The Baroness Altdorff bowed her head in silence.

"It is to clear my dead friend's memory from a foul stigma," continued Saville, "that I have determined to prove his accusers guilty of the vilest conspiracy ever formed. Captain Goddard was accused of cheating at cards at the house of Lord Arlingford."

"But surely," put in Bella-Demonia, "it must have been easy for Captain Goddard to disprove the accusation?"

"There is the mystery. On investigation, there is no doubt that he had a card in his possession which he refused to show. This, in face of the fact that the king of trumps—they were playing écarté—was not to be found, gave color to the charge; though every one knew that Arlingford was quite capable of managing the cards well enough, even if he had been unaided by confederates: he had two on that occasion, a Major Carteret and his sister, Mrs. Bradley Dashton."

"Mrs. Dashton!" said Bella-Demonia. "She is in the house at this moment."

"Here! now?" answered Saville. "May I ask you to say nothing of my mission, and allow me to make my request of you before I meet her?"

"I will see that no one enters," said the prince, rising, and moving towards the door. As he passed Bella-Demonia he said, in an undertone, "I have given orders to Kapiodovitch to have an escort ready to receive our visitor of this evening."

"You make a grave charge against this Lord Arlingford," said she to Dick Saville.

"I am sure of my facts, however,—morally sure. But proof to establish those facts is absolutely necessary. I believe that you, madame, and Prince Schouloff, can help me."

"I? but I never heard of Lord Arlingford."

"It is of Jack Vyvian Fane's career in St. Petersburg that I wish information."

"Vyvian Fane!"

It was more a gasp than an exclamation that broke from the Baroness Altdorff as she spoke the words. Prince Schouloff sat narrowly watching her, a shade of perplexity enveloping his brow.

"You remember him?" asked Saville.

"Remember him!" answered the baroness. "Perfectly. He was the cause of a terrible tragedy, and paid with his life for his treachery."

"You are mistaken, baroness. Vyvian Fane is alive, and is now Lord Arlingford. The title came to him, it is true, very unexpectedly."

"And *this* is the man who ruined Captain Goddard? In St. Petersburg he betrayed an innocent man to death,—a man beloved by all, a man who knew no wrong,—and struck down his wife and child with the self-same blow. Oh, you did well to come to me! I can give you all the information that you want. Listen!"

At this moment a servant entered.

"Your Excellency's secretary has returned," said he to Bella-Demonia.

"Admit him."

The giant form of Rodia Pouschkoff entered the room. Delivering a note to his mistress, he waited whilst she read it, and then, receiving a hurried command in a low tone, left the room once more. The Baroness Altdorff turned to Dick Saville.

"I must ask you to wait until to-morrow," she said, "for the details. A sudden call interrupts us." And she rang for a servant.

"Conduct Mr. and Mrs. Saville to their apartments.—*Au revoir*, Mrs. Saville, and I hope *à bientôt*."

Dick Saville and his wife left the room, accompanied by the servant. When they were gone, Bella-Demonia turned to the prince:

"Beyaz Murad is here, at the gates. Follow me." And she led the way to her own wing of the château.

CHAPTER III.

THE SNARE.

THE boudoir-study of the Baroness Altdorff was a large room opening upon the terrace. When she entered it, accompanied by Prince Schouloff, it was illuminated by a couple of lamps, that served to intensify the gloom beyond the radius of their light.

"This omnipotent general is here," she said, turning to the prince as she closed the door. "I will admit him by this window. Once here, you will have the house surrounded by Kapiodovitch's men, and when I have learnt all I can of his plans I will give a signal. I have my revolver here: I will fire once."

As she spoke she threw open the shutters that guarded the windows, and the light of the rising moon poured into the room; then she came close to the prince, and said, looking him deeply in the eyes,—

"What will you give me for this man's capture?"

"Whatever you choose to ask. What shall it be?"

"*The life of one man, taken or given when and how I shall decide!*"

"Baroness!"

"Don't wonder; don't be surprised: only promise,—promise me by all that you hold holy."

"It shall be as you wish."

"Good! Now go!"

Prince Schouloff left the room, and she listened to his footsteps growing fainter down the corridor.

"At last," said she, as she loosened the fastenings of the window, —"at last I shall be avenged! He lives! How has he escaped all these years? But what does it matter? Ah! how I could have vindicated you, Aubyn Goddard, had *you* too lived! but I can show the world that your honor was stolen from you by a felon; *and I will!*"

She sank into a low chair before the fire, which blazed despite the season, her back turned to the window, her face hidden in her hands.

A slight noise as the window is pushed open from the outside, and a man steps into the room. He is dressed in the simple but striking costume of a Turkish staff-officer. His black military frock is buttoned to the chin, relieved only by the star of the Medjidieh which blazes on the left breast, and thrown into shadow by the folds of his voluminous military cloak. One arm, which is evidently wounded, rests in the breast of his coat, and his feet are cased in high boots which bear the traces of hard and rough riding.

The woman lowers her hands and turns slowly with a little smile upon her face. As their eyes meet, she starts violently and springs to her feet. A cry breaks from her:

"Aubyn Goddard! You! Living! Here, and called Beyaz Murad! What does it mean?"

On his part he is no whit less astounded. He advances towards her:

"The Baroness Altdorff! Is it real? My God! at last I see you again! Is this a dream?"

Quick as thought she has flown to the door and double-locked it, then to the window, which she hastily bars once more. At last she turns and comes to him.

"Would to God we never might waken!" she whispers, in a frightened moan.

As for him, the object of his coming, all, is forgotten in the ecstasy of seeing her again.

"If you only knew," he says, "how often I have prayed that I might live to see you once more! Through all the wild excitement of fighting, *that* hope has been my talisman. I have thought how foolish I was to obey you and not try to find you again in Vienna, till it was too late! When I made up my mind to tell you that I could no longer keep my promise, that I must try to win you back,—that, wild and impetuous as was the dream, its strength swept my reason from me,—ah! I felt that I must return and read once more in your sweet face a promise that——"

"For pity's sake——"

"I sought you too late: you had gone, and left no trace behind. It was a moment of bitter despair, for I thought you would have smiled pardon upon me, and I felt I should not have had to beg in vain. Was I wrong?"

"Oh, forgive me, Aubyn! Why did I not know? Let me speak now."

"Not yet! Let me tell you first, before I touch your lips, that I am ruined, disgraced,—that I have been robbed of name, fame, honor —no! hardly that. But *you* will believe that no fault of mine has exiled me."

"You will break my heart!"

"You have heard how, and why, I left England?"

"Yes,—but just now."

"Do you believe me guilty of the crime of which I was accused?"

"I *know* that you were not, and all the world would have known the same, if you had demanded an explanation."

"And that I could neither demand nor give."

"Oh, you were wrong! You must have been mad not to see how base a suspicion you allowed to take root. Why did you keep silent?"

She had come close to him and laid her hand upon his arm,—the wounded one. He became deathly white, and staggered at her touch.

"What is it?" she exclaimed. "You are ill."

"No, no; it is nothing. Give me some water. Ah! Nothing serious,—only a bit painful. I was wounded a few days ago, and as I was riding here my horse stumbled; I had only one hand, and he threw me. I—I think the wound has opened again. Don't be alarmed: it's all right. It does not pain me now."

He paused and caught his breath.

"It's stupid of me to get knocked over so easily," he continued, "but I've been ill some time, and I suppose that's why I got faint. You were asking me something?"

"Are you better?" she asked, anxiously.

"Yes,—yes. Listen! You asked me why I did not explain how I got that card. I could not. It meant the loss of honor for a woman or for me. The whole thing was a plot, but I could not have proved any conspiracy. This woman was cruelly wronged; I had known her from a child; she was helpless and alone:—can you wonder that I chose even disgrace to save her?"

"But she was wrong to let you do so. How could she keep silent and let you ruin yourself? It was cruel!"

"Don't blame her; she was not to blame, and it can do no good now. I only tell you this because I could not bear that a thought of suspicion should be between us. I had a card on which she had written a message,—innocent enough in itself, but which those who sought to entrap us both could have made to appear guilty. *This* is the secret of my crime. Do you believe me?"

"As I believe in God!"

"My darling!"

They were in each other's arms, the world forgetting in the glory of the moment that they knew each other's love.

"And you will tell me that there is nothing to prevent you resting here upon my heart forever. The war can't last much longer, and I shall be free. Then will you help me to forget the weary time before I knew you? Ah!"

The cry was wrung from him by his agony.

"Ah! you are badly hurt! you are hiding it from me!" she said.

"It is true," he gasped: "the wound is deep, and I am more hurt than I thought. It's only the loss of blood, however. Don't come near. It will frighten you."

At that moment a slight noise upon the terrace outside struck her ear, and recalled her to the present. It was the light clank of a rifle as it touched the gravel.

"My God!" she exclaimed, "there is danger here. You must try to keep strong,—to get away. Heaven forgive me! you are betrayed! Can't you walk? Try. Come here into my room: it is your only chance of safety."

Her words and tone recalled him too to his senses.

"Why are you here?" he said; "and where is the woman I came to see?—Bella-Demonia? I don't understand."

"Don't try to understand. I will tell you when you are safe. Come with me."

"What do you mean? I can't——"

A footstep in the corridor. Quick as thought the woman seized his wounded arm, and with the pain he fell senseless to the ground. Then she fired her revolver,—twice. A knock on the door! She drew his pistol from its holster and laid it on the floor, drawing his cloak over his face as she did so. With a crash the door fell open, and Prince Schouloff entered the room.

"For God's sake get help!" she exclaimed. "When he found he was betrayed he would have killed me. I shot him. He was going to escape. I tried to keep him: he was desperate—then I fired. *He is dead!*"

"I was wrong to let you risk such an interview," said the prince, looking at the prostrate form. "I will see myself that no one enters till he is taken away."

He was moving to the door. Then he turned and came back. "Perhaps he is only wounded," he said, laying his hand upon the senseless man's heart. He was just going once more, when he saw the revolver on the floor. He picked it up and pointed it at the still form.

"Better make quite sure!" he said.

He was about to fire, when Bella-Demonia flung herself upon the body.

"No! no!" she cried, "I have lied to you! I have betrayed you both!"

The cloak fell from Goddard's features. The prince looked at him.

"Captain Goddard!" he exclaimed.

"Yes, yes! It is Captain Goddard. Listen! For this man's capture you promised me the life of one man given or taken how and when I should decide. *I claim his!*"

CHAPTER IV.

FACE TO FACE.

FOR the next few days the inhabitants of the Villa Kristov Hisar lived in a state of suppressed excitement. Prince Schouloff's first care was to send Mrs. Dashton off to Nice, armed with all that was needful to bring Lord Arlingford back to London, but ignorant of what had taken place at the villa. Of the amazement of Dick Saville and his wife it is unnecessary to speak. Kitty and the Baroness Altdorff relieved each other in the care of Goddard, who woke from his swoon in a high delirium.

The prince said but little, biding his time and waiting for Bella-Demonia to speak.

At last, one day when Goddard was fairly convalescent, she sent for him to her boudoir. She was sitting listlessly before the fire when he entered, and, looking up, gave him her hand, which he respectfully kissed.

"Be seated, prince," she said. "The time has come when some explanation is due to you. I wish to give it to you now."

"You are not overtaxing your strength, baroness?"

"No. I am as eager to question as I am willing to answer."

"I am all attention."

"Had you any suspicion that Beyaz Murad Bey and Aubyn Goddard were one and the same man?"

"Not the faintest."

" You believed him to be dead?"

" Implicitly."

" What has been the result of his detention here?"

" The result has been the beginning of the end. The Flying Legion, suddenly deprived of its leader, has lost its position as an independent army corps. Radetzky and Gourko have at last defeated Suleiman, and the Russian standard floats in the Shipka Pass. Suleiman is trying to regain his position, but in vain. Meanwhile, Skobeleff refuses to take warning from July, or advice from Todleben, and is preparing to attack Plevna once more, now that Osman's reinforcements have been stopped."

" It has been a great work," said the baroness, drearily.

" For which a great price has been paid, baroness."

" A great price?"

" The life of Captain Goddard given and taken when and how you decided," said Schouloff.

" Ah! it was fortunate for Lord Arlingford, his betrayer, that it was so! Had it not been Goddard's it would have been his."

" You have plunged me in a whirl of wonder, baroness. The afternoon that Mr. and Mrs. Saville arrived you expressed your ignorance of Viscount Arlingford. Five minutes later the sound of his name caused you the first strong emotion that I have ever known you to betray. It is with John Vyvian Fane that you are concerned,— John Vyvian Fane, now Viscount Arlingford. You have cause to hate him. Tell me about it: I can help you, and I will."

" You?"

" Even so. Lord Arlingford was at one time in the employ of the secret police in Petersburg——"

" I know!"

" He was expelled for making it the instrument of a private vengeance——"

" I know!"

" He implicated an innocent man in the socialist schemes of one Dorski——"

" I know!"

" You know! you know!" exclaimed Schouloff. " How do you know?"

" You ask me how I know. You ask me why I have sworn an oath of vengeance against this Lord Arlingford, once John Vyvian Fane. Ask me rather the question you have spent time and money in vain to have answered: ask me rather who I am."

" My God! what do you mean?"

" *I am the Princess Carita Galitzin!*"

" Holy St. Katerine!"

Prince Schouloff rose and went successively to the doors leading into the corridor, and into Bella-Demonia's apartments, to make sure against eavesdroppers.

Then he returned to her side, and, bending till his eyes were plunged in hers, he took her wrist in his soft irresistible grasp and said, in a low, distinct voice,—

"*And I am Alexis Dorski !*"

* * * * * * * *

For some minutes a dead silence reigned in the room.

The Princess Galitzin, to call her by her real name, had sprung to her feet, pressing her hands to her throbbing temples, as she looked down at the man who, after intrusting her with the master-secret of his life, had resumed his seat calmly.

"The mystery of the cipher-dial is at last explained," said·Schouloff at length.

"And his son,—Dmitri Dmitrievitch Keratieff,—does he know?"

"No one knows, save the Princess Galitzin, and Schouloff, the Chief of Police."

"Why have you told me?"

"You have a letter of mine."

"True: here it is." And, rapidly unfastening the bosom of her dress, she took therefrom a tightly-folded paper, which, opening, she laid before him.

"That is your handwriting?" she said.

"No; it *was* the handwriting of Alexis Dorski the Terrorist. It was missing from among the secret papers of Keratieff. It was to obtain it that, primarily, I obtained his position. I have sought it ever since. It was to obtain it that I made his son my confidential secretary. Had I known in whose hands it lay, I should have rested easy."

"It is at your service. Now !"

"Now?"

"Tell me: Vyvian Fane was reported assassinated on the Polish frontier."

"True; but it was his valet who was murdered and mutilated beyond recognition. His connection with the Third Section gave him means of learning the conspiracy against him. He boarded an English cruiser which lay off the Fortress of the Schlusselburg. Arrived in England, the unexpected reversion of the title and estates of Arlingford served more completely to conceal him : the name of Vyvian Fane was dropped. I alone of the Department have kept track of his lordship, and I have surrounded him with such a net-work that when the time comes to strike, he cannot escape me !"

"Cannot escape *you ?*"

"Yes, me. Over the senseless form of your brother's wife I swore to avenge my friend Ladislas Galitzin. It was *I* who apprised you of her condition that fatal night. Since then I have made Arlingford my tool in many a plot, only the more surely to shatter him when I turn down my thumbs and cry, like the Romans in the arena, '*Habet !*' "

"When shall you strike ?"

"As soon as the war is over and Captain Goddard can return with us to London. I have sent Mrs. Dashton to take him thither supplied with the necessary funds to bring him within our grasp. I summoned her here to obtain information of Captain Goddard's death. I confess to you that I would have given ten years of my life to get it; for then I dreamed that perhaps you—well, well, that is over now. I will show you that I am grateful to 'Bella-Demonia.' I will show you that though I cannot be your lover I can still be your friend and ally, and my power is as much yours as it would be were you mine. No, not a word! I do not wear my heart upon my sleeve, but, princess, I love you more than I shall ever tell you. Now! it is over. There! we will change the subject."

The princess had risen as he spoke. When he became silent she moved to his side, and, sinking on her knees beside him, she took his hand in hers. A strong shudder passed across his frame, as the woman bent and pressed her lips to his hand and a hot tear fell upon it.

Then, as she raised her head and looked at him, he bent his reverently, and for the first and last time kissed the marble-cold brow that was upturned to him.

BOOK IV.

CHAPTER I.

SOWING THE WIND.

WHEN our story reopens in the month of April, 1878, great changes —almost cataclysms—have occurred in Europe. The Treaty of San Stefano has been signed, and the Powers, waking to the enormity of its conditions, are preparing for the Congress of Berlin. What might have been the end of the Turko-Russian war of 1877–78 had the Flying Legion succeeded in reaching Osman Pasha, it is impossible to surmise. The dispersal of that mysterious organization seemed to mark the turning-point of the war. Osman's last supplies reached him from Sofia in November, and on the 9th of December, driven to despair, he made his heroic and historic sortie, which would have undoubtedly been successful had not treachery from within the bastions of Plevna apprised Todleben of his intention, and enabled the Russian general, at the cost of the Siberian regiment, to force the surrender, with all the honors of war, of the greatest soldier that Turkey had known since the days of Mahmoud the Reformer. New Year's day, 1878, saw Gourko across the Etropol Balkans, and on Twelfth-Night he supped in Sofia. At the end of the month Adrianople was reached, and a British fleet entered the Bosphorus under a protest which England's Greatest Statesman utterly disregarded.

In this way was Constantinople saved the ignominy of becoming a Russian watering-place.

Meanwhile, the actors in our drama had reassembled in London, where the last act was to be played out. Goddard had recovered from the effects of his wound only after months of patient nursing on the part of his soul's idol. Lord Arlingford had returned to town, and Prince Schouloff, present ostensibly on diplomatic service, was shifting the strings of the web he had drawn around his victim, from finger to finger, as the development of events required.

Our story reopens in the little drawing-room of Mrs. Bradley Dashton's cosey *maisonnette* in Mayfair. Two men are present, one pacing irritably up and down, the other comfortably ensconced in an arm-chair.

The first is Viscount Arlingford, the second is that promising soldier of the army of financial martyrs, Major Homer Carteret. Lord Arlingford comes suddenly to a full stop.

"Why the deuce," says he, "did you let Emily come back to England, least of all at this most critical juncture? You know how impetuous she is, and among the ways out of our present difficulties you know very well that there is no choice."

"And you know very well, my dear Arlingford, that I can't control her any more than you can. She appeared to come to the decision in an instant, and declined to allow me to argue the point. I've always warned you that she would be dangerous if the spirit so moved her, and yet you allowed the Briggs affair to get into print. Indeed, it was sheer folly of you to make the running in that direction at all."

"You put the case charmingly, my dear Carteret, only you seem to forget that at the time I went for the little Briggs there was no other course open,—indeed, that it is only within the last twenty-four hours that circumstances have permitted me to drop her out at all. Another trifle that you overlook is that neither you nor I could have foreseen the extraordinary turn affairs have taken. I shall be able now to pay all my debts and start for Algiers as soon as possible."

"That is, supposing Emily to be tractable."

"You leave me to manage her : she's not likely to give me much trouble. What a time she is ! I shall be late. I promised to go and look at a horse : they tell me he's a clipper, and up to my weight, —can jump anything. Look here ! I wish you'd go down to Rice's and tell him I can't come till to-morrow, but that if his horse is all he says he is, I'll take him."

"But I thought you said you were going to Algiers ?" remarked Major Carteret, with an interrogative inflection.

"Yes, so I am. But I fancy I can win a bit steeple-chasing before I go. Featherstone, who's ordered out to India, has offered me a couple of horses that have been running wonderfully well at some of the small meetings. He only wants three hundred and fifty pounds for 'em,—dirt-cheap. The three will do me very well ; and when I go I'll give you the lot, if you like, and you can hunt this year."

"Thanks, old man," replied Carteret, rising. "I'll go and inspect my future property; but, egad! I'm afraid my creditors will do most of the hunting."

"Oh! all right. Say they're still mine. Good-by. Be in time to-night."

"Yes. Good-by."

And his lordship was left alone. Not for long, however, for a moment later Mrs. Dashton entered the room.

"Aren't you glad to see me, Jack ?" she said, advancing with both hands outstretched. "I've so much to forgive you that—I daren't begin. Suppose I absolve you blind, without going into the details. Tell me, weren't you surprised to know that I was here ?"

"Yes,—deucedly surprised. And I wish you hadn't come."

"How horrid of you to say that! and it's such a long time since I've seen you, too, you bad boy!"

She had come up behind him and put her hands on his shoulders as he sat. He disengaged himself a trifle impatiently.

"My dear girl," he said, "I wish you wouldn't do this. You know it bores me. You shouldn't have come over: you'll upset all my plans. Why didn't you stop in Paris?"

"Because I am fool enough to care for you, and weak enough to believe you cared a little for me. But don't place too much reliance on my folly. I tell you, Jack, that the day I make up my mind that you mean to throw me over, it will be a bad day for you!" She had come close to him, and her tone changed from one of intense earnestness to one of ugly cynicism. "I'm afraid you'll make me lose my temper. Don't! I'm not nice when I'm angry."

"Now, look here, Emily: this tragic tone is out of place. You know it's no use acting with me."

"When I do *act* with you, it will be forcibly enough to claim your attention; but before that happens, I want you to explain one or two things. I came here expecting that you would be glad to see me. I didn't believe the stories I heard about an American girl; and now I want to know from you how much truth there was in them. That you would be unscrupulous enough to deceive me I don't doubt, but that you would be fool enough to arouse my enmity I doubt very much. But, bah! I didn't come to England to threaten. Are you going to marry the girl?"

"No!"

Mrs. Dashton heaved a sigh of relief.

"Ah! I was sure of you," she said. "Why do you try to make me jealous? You shouldn't do it, Jack,—you shouldn't do it. Well, the trouble of the journey is well repaid, now that the suspense is over. Of course I *knew* it wasn't true; yet I couldn't rest until I was sure."

"Now, look here, Emily," exclaimed Arlingford, rising to his feet: "let us put an end to this. I'm going back to my wife."

"What! You're not in earnest?"

"I am,—perfectly."

"Very well! so am I. *You shan't do it!*"

"Don't talk nonsense, but listen to me. An aunt of my wife's has left her her fortune and advised her to make friends with me. You don't suppose I am going to chuck away such an opportunity,—especially as everything is as bad as it can be at home? My agent can't get me a penny. Now make up your mind to accept the situation. I'll go to Paris as soon as I can; meanwhile, I'll see you get all the money you want——"

"Do you suppose," broke in the woman indignantly, "that I am the kind of woman to be ordered about?—to be a pensioner on your *wife's* bounty? Undeceive yourself! It's your turn to listen to *me*. I would have endured any privation for you and with you—for love. That is over: you make it a business transaction. Very well: you must accept *my* terms. I have disgraced myself long enough for you. You will marry *me*."

"Don't be a fool," was the brutal response. "One must draw the line somewhere, and I couldn't fly in the face of the world as far as *that*. I have a few friends I must consider, and——"

"So! I am not good enough for you,—you, who cannot enter a decent house in England,—you, the sharper,—the thief! Do you forget I know how you ruined Goddard?"

"I don't care a damn what you know. I was willing to take care of you; you refuse help. *Soit!* A woman who lets a married man make love to her always gets the worst of it in the long run. I am going to become respectable, and in five years no one will remember that I was ever anything else. You might have known, as I didn't ask you to come, that I didn't want you——"

He was cut short by the entrance of a servant with a note. Mrs. Dashton tore it open and glanced through it, visibly excited. Hastily writing a few words at her *escritoire*, she handed the answer to the servant, who left the room. Mrs. Dashton appeared to have recovered all her composure.

"I thought we knew each other pretty well," she said, "but it appears that we are both destined to make discoveries. Your new fad for respectability is a little startling. My determination may be equally astonishing. I simply decline to take the place you assign to me."

"My dear Emily, the great charm about you *was*, that you were so thoroughly sensible. You are not like yourself to-day. I've told you what I mean to do."

"In other words, you defy me. Now I'll tell you what *I* mean to do. I can't make you marry me, but you certainly shan't marry anybody else. I have helped you in your dirty work, I have done things for your sake that no money in the world would have induced me to do, and if you suppose that you can calmly say, 'Good-by, I've no further use for you,' and expect that that is the end, you are vastly mistaken. So your idea of a sensible woman—such as you are good enough to call me—is one who is always ready to subscribe to your pleasure or income as necessity demands? So long as her *sense* is used for your benefit, she is charming, but you are always surprised when she exerts it in her own behalf. I *will* be sensible, and mind you don't regret it. So I am to wander away an outcast,—*déclassée*,—whilst you become a respectable member of society? Charming!"

As she spoke, Lord Arlingford had risen, and, taking his hat and cane, had moved to the door. Seeing him on the point of departure, she ran to him and flung her arms about him.

"Oh, Jack, Jack," she cried, "don't go like that! I was only desperate. Say you did not mean what you said. You don't really mean to throw me over, after all your promises?"

"I've said all I have to say," answered the man, roughly. "Let me go. You know 'scenes' bore me. Let me go, I say!"

He flung her from him, and went out. Her foot catching on some piece of furniture, she fell heavily to the ground. For a moment she lay as if dazed; then a great sob escaped her, and with difficulty she rose and staggered to her writing-table. Her eyes fell upon the note that lay where she had left it.

"Ah, Jack," she said, aloud, "if you had known who was waiting an answer to this letter, you would have been more—more discreet."

She touched a bell, and the next moment Captain Aubyn Goddard entered the room.

"I am glad you are here," she said, recovering herself as she went to meet him. "You have been very kind to me,—much kinder than I deserve, for until this moment I had no intention of repaying you."

"Poor old lady!" answered Goddard, soothingly. "Why, how upset you are! What has happened? Can I do anything to help you?"

"Always the same kindly sympathy, Aubyn. How good you are! I see by this note you came over to get a confession from Jack Arlingford. You want my help. You value this vindication very much, do you not?"

"Of course I do. Until his confession is obtained, there may be those who doubt me; and, more than the opinion of all, there is one whose faith in me must be justified. There is to be a meeting to-night at Briggs's to endeavor to bring it about, and you can help it, I know. You've known me for years, old girl, and you know I was innocent, don't you?"

"More! I will prove it. But you must go now, for I expect a visitor. Give me the address of your friend where the explanation is to take place, and you shall have proof,—all the proof you want. And don't judge me too harshly for my share in the matter: I have had but one excuse,—I did it for him. And just now he struck me down!—Oh!"

"He struck you!"

"Yes."

"My God! What a brute!"

"Never mind now: you must go. I—I am engaged. But we shall meet to-night."

Goddard left her. When she was alone, she moved once more to her desk, and, opening a locked drawer, took from it an envelope, at which she gazed for a few moments motionless.

Then hurriedly she tore it open and took from it a playing-card.

It was the king of clubs.

CHAPTER II.

THE VENGEANCE OF THREE WOMEN.

As she stood looking at it, the servant entered, bearing a card on a salver. She took it up with an air of lazy indifference which quickly changed to one of strong emotion.

"Lady Arlingford!" she exclaimed; then, turning to the servant, she added, "You did not say that I was in?"

"No, ma'am," answered the domestic. "I said that I would see."

"Say, not at home." Then, as the servant was leaving the room, she added, "Stay !"

She stood, twirling the piece of pasteboard in her fingers.

"What can she want of me,—that woman,—here in my house?" Then, apparently making up her mind, she hastily concealed the playing-card in the bosom of her dress, and said, "Show her in."

Lady Arlingford entered the room, and the two women bowed without speaking.

"You are surprised to see me," said Lady Arlingford, recovering herself the first. "I owe you, perhaps, an apology for intruding upon you, but I felt that I must come. I—I have a favor to ask."

The concluding words were spoken with an obvious effort, and Mrs. Dashton, with an inclination of her head, signified that she was listening.

"You have heard that there is to be a meeting to-night for the exoneration of Captain Goddard?" said her ladyship.

"Yes."

"You will be there?"

"Yes."

"I—I—you have heard that I desire to re-marry Lord Arlingford?"

"I have heard it."

"Mrs. Dashton, it is better to speak plainly. I know that Lord Arlingford's position in the matter will depend greatly on what you will say. I know what your feelings under the circumstances must be. I hope—I believe—that he will make every possible reparation. I have come to beg that you will hold your hand so far as you can."

"What do you wish me to do?"

"Am I right in supposing that your evidence can ruin his lordship?—I mean, in the matter of the card?"

For all answer Mrs. Bradley Dashton slowly drew the king of clubs from its resting-place and laid it on the table.

As Lady Arlingford's eyes fell upon it, she exclaimed,—

"It is as I feared. I have come to beg that you will not confront him with that card. It will be my care that Captain Goddard shall produce the card which he actually held,—the one on which I wrote. Will you not be merciful?—will you not shield my husband so far as not to add this horrible evidence to mine?"

"Lady Arlingford," returned Mrs. Dashton, "you have been frank with me; I will be equally so with you. An hour ago I would have guarded this card with my life; but within this hour things have altered."

"But surely——"

"No ! let me think."

Her reflections were interrupted by the re-entrance of the servant.

"The Baroness Altdorff is below," said he to his mistress, in a low tone.

"Ask her to come here," said Mrs. Dashton; then, turning to the suppliant woman before her, she said,—

"A lady is below, who calls by appointment. On what she will say my decision must in a great measure depend. If you will step into this next room, I will tell you what that decision is when she has left me."

"You say that she can influence you: will you not let me try to influence her? A woman should be merciful to one of her sex."

"Perhaps. At present I cannot tell. Step in here, however, and in ten minutes you shall know."

There was no time for parley, and the Countess of Arlingford stepped into the adjoining boudoir. Mrs. Bradley Dashton stood looking at the card that lay upon the table.

"Ah," said she, as if apostrophizing the pasteboard, "I wonder into whose hands you will eventually fall? Those two men and that woman who have just left this room would give a good deal for you, and Bella-Demonia wants you more than either of them. Ah, baroness, you want my assistance in unmasking Lord Arlingford! You little know how much I can serve you, and how willingly I will do so."

The next moment Bella-Demonia was announced.

"You are punctual, baroness," said Mrs. Dashton, coming forward. "That is good, for it seems we have much to do. You will believe, I am sure, that I appreciate the confidence you have reposed in me, and I will justify it."

"You have already justified it by guarding the secret of Captain Goddard's identity with the Turkish general who reached the Villa Kristov Hisar just before you left us."

"But I never knew it until after Lord Arlingford had left me in Paris and returned to London."

"It was as well, we thought, that you should get some suspicion of what kind of man this Arlingford really is, before you knew so important a secret. You know, we women, when we love——"

"Yes, yes; I know all that you would say. Your letter of yesterday tells me I can help you further."

"Yes; and I trust we may count upon you?"

"I know what you want, and—yes, you may count upon me. I will meet you to-night at Mr. Briggs's in Hereford Street at nine o'clock, and, believe me, Goddard will have no more valuable ally there than Emily Dashton."

"I supposed," said Bella-Demonia, "that I should have had a hard fight to gain your aid. I will not ask why you are so unexpectedly won over, but I want you to know that my gratitude shall be no empty form of words. I will endeavor to prove to you how I value your sacrifice. May I speak frankly?"

Mrs. Dashton had seated herself in the low arm-chair, and bowed her head silently. The other woman continued:

"Captain Goddard's vindication must be in a great measure due to you and what you will say. I know that the words which will give joy to us will bring pain and grief to you. Mrs. Dashton, I can't be a humbug, and it is not for me to preach to you. The part you have played in the drama which is to end to-night will cost you many a pang. You are a woman, alone in your struggle with life. I should like you to feel that you can always count on one woman who will sympathize with, will assist, and, if necessary, protect you, and that that woman is she whom you have known as Bella-Demonia."

Mrs. Dashton had not raised her eyes.

" Don't give me too much credit for speaking the truth to-night."

" I can see that you are much upset. Let me beg you to take a little rest now. I will send my carriage for you at nine o'clock."

" Thank you. I will be ready."

" I suppose I am right in thinking that you still possess the card that Lord Arlingford gave you to conceal,—to destroy?"

Mrs. Dashton pointed to the table.

" There it is !" she said.

" Ah! you will give it me?" said Bella-Demonia, eagerly.

Mrs. Dashton smiled.

" In that room a woman awaits your departure to renew a request she has made to me. She also desires this card, that she may destroy it."

" A woman?—who?"

" The Countess of Arlingford."

" No? I am most anxious to meet Lady Arlingford in this way, informally," said she, eagerly. " You would oblige me very much by asking her to come in here, and by presenting us to each other."

" I should like to do as you wish, but I am afraid to trust myself in such a meeting."

" If you will do as I ask and make some excuse to leave us together for a short time, I promise you that you shall be spared the embarrassment of ever meeting her again."

" You are mysterious as usual, baroness, but I know if you promise, that you can perform, and I will do as you wish. Is there anything in particular that you wish me to say?"

" No; only, as soon as you can, make some excuse and leave us."

" Certainly. And by what name do you wish me to present you?"

" By my own."

" The Baroness Altdorff?"

" No; the Princess Galitzin."

" What !"

" That is my real name, which you and Prince Schouloff alone have heard."

There was no time to express her surprise, as Mrs. Dashton opened the door of the boudoir and the Countess of Arlingford entered the room.

" Lady Arlingford," said Mrs, Dashton, " let me present you to a friend. The Princess Galitzin—Lady Arlingford."

The two women bowed to each other.

" I must be going immediately," said Bella-Demonia. " I think my carriage must be back."

" If you will excuse me, I will go and see," said Mrs. Dashton. " I have some orders to give."

And she left them together.

" I think, Lady Arlingford," began the Princess Galitzin, " that we have a mutual friend in Captain Goddard. I may tell you that I shall be present at the meeting which is to take place to-night. It will be painful to you, but at least it will have the advantage of proving the innocence of our friend."

"You know him? Oh, I am so glad!" replied Lady Arlingford. "I think he is the embodiment of all that is honest and true in man. I had, alas! the misfortune of doing him the greatest wrong that was ever done——"

"I am sure you exaggerate your share," put in the princess, gently.

"Of course I was innocent of the intention, but the result is the same. It seems so hard that after bearing my burden for so long I should have broken down at that moment, as you know. Just as I was about to tell how I had given him the card, I became insensible. I never shall forget the horror of that moment. I could have exonerated Aubyn with a word, and that word I could not speak. I tried—I fought, it seemed to me, for hours, till the blank of insensibility came over me. Oh, it was cruel!"

"Are you not afraid of overtaxing your strength, Lady Arlingford? Would it not be wiser to avoid such an explanation as must take place to-night? Your friends might represent you, and save you much pain."

"No, I must be present, for a reason so strong that nothing can overcome it. It is not alone to vindicate my old friend that I go. I go to intercede for one who will find no defenders,—one who I feel is so alone that his need has won my sympathy,—my husband!"

"You can plead for him? But he is no longer your husband: you are divorced."

"He is my child's father: what divorce of law can alter that? You will think that I am very weak, but I have my own opinions. There is nothing of the Bohemian in my disposition."

"Bohemian! May I ask what you call 'Bohemian'? You do not answer. Let me define it for you. It is something distinct from 'a lady.' A lady means one who is well born, tenderly nurtured, carefully educated; always placed—that is, presumably placed—beyond the knowledge of evil, she is sheltered from contact with the sufferings and sorrows of her less fortunate sisters. The woman who enjoys these advantages is called a lady,—a title which signifies, not the individual, but the manner of her training. A Bohemian, as you intend it, means one who is outside the pale of respectability, an object of suspicion, one whom you only consent to meet when she can be of service to you. Yet I have known many 'ladies' the names of whose lovers are better known than the inner life of the reigning Bohemian. You would be surprised to know that Bohemians look down on certain sections of 'society' in amazement and pity."

"You have evidently made your experiences in unfortunate examples," replied Lady Arlingford. "Do you not believe that there are ladies who are good women?"

"God forbid that I should not! There is a sweet old-world title that brings to my mind all that is noble and good in womanhood,—a title that lives in my heart, shrouded in reverence,—a title that fits the beings who have rendered the name of mother sacred. That title is 'gentlewoman.' *That* title I believe in, and it is found in Bohemia as well as in society."

"These are strange expressions for the Princess Galitzin, who can know but little of these people except by force of imagination."

"You are mistaken. *My* flag bears the red and white of Bohemia, and has seen good service, believe me. Perhaps you will understand me better if I tell you that *I am called Bella-Demonia.*"

"Bella-Demonia!" Lady Arlingford had risen to her feet.

"You appear shocked," said the Princess Galitzin.

"I am a little startled, I confess. I was not prepared to meet so—so—public—a character."

"And you would not have cared to meet me, if you had known who I was. Would you?"

"I will admit—as I do not share your opinions—that I should have refused to meet the bearer of the name ' Bella-Demonia:' a meeting would not be pleasant for either of us. Still, I feel bound to say that you are quite different from what I should have expected."

"Thank you for your generous admission : you are good enough to imply that there is nothing in my appearance or manner to deprive me of the inestimable boon of at least *looking* presentable. You are a good woman and capable of noble impulses, but charity for your fellow-women seems to be no part of your creed. Is it ignorance or intolerance that makes you condemn without even one expression of regret a woman of whom you know nothing?"

"Nothing? I have heard——"

"Heard? I said *know.*"

"Pardon me for reminding you that you have only yourself to blame for the impression formed of you. If a woman has no husband, and yet——"

"If respectability is based upon the possession of a husband, then I am worthy of your highest esteem. Lady Arlingford, I am about to tell you a story which may—I hope will—interest you."

Her ladyship bent her head, and the princess continued :

"My mother died when I was very young. I lived with my father at our château in the province of Ladoga, alone save for the companionship of a young girl, the daughter of a serf mother. She was my companion and friend rather than my attendant, and we were romantic and impressionable, both of us. One day we had wandered far from the château, among the woods. We were about to return home, when a crashing in the bushes announced the presence of some large animal. An instant later one of our mountain bears bounded into the clearing. We clung to each other almost senseless with terror, when suddenly we heard the report of a rifle close to us, and the beast fell dead. A moment after, a man sprang through the bushes, congratulating us on our escape, and apologizing for his sudden apparition and the alarm he had caused us. He escorted us home, and was welcomed by my father, the more warmly when it transpired that he was of good family. He was an Englishman, on a hunting-tour, he said. He was staying close by, and became a constant visitor at the house. The sequel is—*banale.* I fancied myself in love. My brother, to whom the stranger was personally antipathetic, had contracted a secret marriage with my late companion, and they had gone to Petersburg, where my brother was commissioned in our Regiment of the Transfiguration. Left alone, we were not long in following my brother's example: we were married secretly, on account of my father, whose pride of race was worthy of a Galitzin, and in the winter the family moved to Petersburg. There my brother's suspicions were aroused, and, determined to drive this Englishman from Petersburg, he sought an opportunity of quarrelling with him. One night there was a terrible scandal at the Club. My brother accused my husband of cheating, and a meeting was arranged. Late that night he caused my brother's arrest. Oh, in my unhappy country it is not difficult to rob a man of liberty and even life on the merest suspicion! I will spare you my tears, my distraction, and give you the facts briefly. I learnt that my brother had been denounced by my husband. He was doomed. I never saw him again: *he died.* When it is inconvenient to substantiate a charge against a political prisoner in Russia, he has a convenient way of dying. From that moment I had but one thought, but one passion,—revenge! My husband was expelled the country, and on the frontier his carriage was wrecked by bandits, and himself —as I thought—assassinated. I sought oblivion of my wrongs and plunged into the sea of politics. I became Prince Schouloff's most able lieutenant. In a word, I became 'Bella-Demonia.' My desperation made me famous; but, though employed by the government, my sympathies were always with the oppressed, and many a life have I saved when it has been to all intents and purposes doomed. But why continue? Even such feverish excitement as mine becomes wearisome, and just when I was most weary I met Captain Goddard. For the first time I felt glad that I had been spared the commission of a crime, that my hands were innocent of my husband's blood."

As she finished speaking, Lady Arlingford rose.

"You have forced me to listen to a discourse," said she, coldly, "that cannot possibly concern me and can only be painful to yourself."

"You will change your opinion," answered the Princess Galitzin. "I told you this story to illustrate the point of our discussion. I tell you it is well for you that all people do not gauge a woman's virtue by the possession of a husband; for *you* have never had one, and are unfortunate enough to be the mother of a child not born in wedlock."

"I! How dare you——"

"How dare I? Why, the man who murdered my brother and with him his wife and unborn child, the man whom I hounded hungry for his life, is alive! Because the man you think to be your husband *is mine!*"

"My God! it is not true!—it cannot be true!"

"I tell you that the man who robbed me of name and dignity, of my very birthright of gentlewoman, who made of me a character for such women as you to sneer at, is alive. He *was* John Vyvian Fane; he *is* Viscount Arlingford."

"Ah, you are only saying this because I offended you. I did not mean to be so cruel. See, I kneel to you to ask you for the truth. Will you swear to me that what you have said is true or untrue?"

"It is true, so help me God! And I will prove it."

When Mrs. Dashton entered the room, Lady Arlingford lay senseless at the feet of the princess.

CHAPTER III.

WEAVING THE WEB.

WHEN, half an hour later, the Princess Galitzin entered her rooms at her hotel, she found Prince Schouloff seated, patiently awaiting her arrival.

"I came to tell you," said he, rising to meet her as she entered, "that there are new complications, of which you are ignorant, and which it would be well for you to know."

"Well?"

"Lord Arlingford's position with regard to his wife is considerably altered since yesterday."

"I think not."

Schouloff looked at her critically for a moment, and then resumed:

"I learn that her ladyship is willing to forget and forgive everything, and proposes to be re-married to him."

"You are wrong in your facts, prince," answered she, with a hardly perceptible smile. "Lady Arlingford is *not* willing to forget or to forgive, and she has no intention of re-marrying him, for she has never been divorced."

For a brief moment it flashed across the prince that the woman's mind was wandering; but, if so, her placid smile belied the fact. He contented himself with answering simply,—

"I do not understand you: you speak in riddles."

"Of which you would like to have the solution."

"Where is that solution to be obtained?" queried the prince, patiently.

"Why, of Lady Arlingford, of course."

"I should like to see her," said Schouloff, reflectively. "Do you think she can receive me at this time?"

"I am sure she will be charmed, prince."

"And where is she now?—can you tell me?"

"Here."

"Here! Where?"

"In this room,—before you."

"In heaven's name, what do you mean?"

"I am she."

The words were said simply as the princess dropped into a chair.

For a minute not a word was said. Then the prince sprang to his feet and exclaimed,—

"I see it all! You married this man in Russia, did you not?"

"Yes."

"It was thus that he had access to your apartments and stole—my letter?"

"Exactly."

"Does any one else know of this? Of course not."

"Yes. I have seen the woman he pretended to marry this afternoon, and I told her. It was time."

"How did she take it?"

"As you might suppose."

"Well, what are you going to do about it?"

"It is the last weapon I hold in reserve to compel Arlingford to confess his share in the plot that ruined Goddard. Until that confession is obtained, I hold my rights over his head. Once Goddard is free, the annulment of our marriage is an easy task; the time that has elapsed, the circumstances,—everything will assist; and *you* would require no assistance."

The prince had been standing staring into the fireplace. Now he turned, and, looking her full in the eyes, he said, calmly,—

"And then?"

She blushed violently, and answered not a word.

"Never mind," continued the prince. "I have shown you that I have your happiness, rather than mine, at heart: I will prove it yet further to you. We shall meet at Mr. Briggs's at half-past nine. In spite of the snares we have tangled around the feet of Arlingford, he may yet brazen his way out, at least temporarily. I will come prepared with the last and most coercive resource, which we have in the Russian police."

"You will dare?—here in England?"

"You forget that John Vyvian Fane was a duly-enrolled member of the Third Section?"

"Forget it!"

"Well, though no formal extradition treaty exists, the arm of His Majesty the Tzar is long enough to reach his servants, wherever they may be. Leave it to me."

"Willingly. Till to-night, then?"

"*Au revoir.*"

CHAPTER IV.

AN AMERICAN CITIZEN.

It was shortly after eight o'clock, and Mr. Cincinnatus Q. Briggs sat at his table in the library of his house in Hereford Street, busily engaged in writing.

From the point of view of the ordinary English novelist, whose knowledge of the American gentleman is bounded on the East by his steamer acquaintance with the travelling salesman and on the West by the charming stories of Bret Harte, added to the occasional "gun" stories of more or less inventive bar-room loafers, whose daily bread—or, more accurately speaking, whose daily whiskey—is obtained by their ability to amuse the crowd, Mr. Cincinnatus Q. Briggs was a most disappointing American. His rooms were furnished with the tasteful simplicity of a scholarly traveller's den. The carpets were unsullied by promiscuous expectoration, the walls were decorated with a few proof etchings

and here and there a masterpiece in aquarelle; there were no carica-
tures of colored deacons, nor were there portraits of fast trotters and
the whiskers of Mr. Vanderbilt to be seen. With the exception of a
small revolver which lay in one of the pigeon-holes of the desk, there
was not a "gun" of any kind to be found, the arms and legs of the
furniture had not been whittled into fanciful designs under the bowie
of their owner, and the paraphernalia of cocktail-manufacture were
conspicuous by their absence.

Mr. Briggs laid down his pen, and, leaning back in his chair,—
which, by the bye, he did not tilt upon its hinder legs,—took up the
letter which he had just completed.

"I think that this will do," said he to himself, as he read over his
composition :

"MY DEAR MR. SAVILLE,—

"I regret to say that Lord Arlingford refuses to avail himself of
the opportunity of flight. He has evidently some strong weapon in
reserve. He means to fight; and, unless yours are stronger, I fear my
stupid cousin will succeed in ruining her life. He is a clever scoundrel,
and has adopted the surest means of making her his defender, by affect-
ing to confide in her all that is detrimental to him, and so cutting the
ground from under every one else's feet. I send you this as arranged,
that you may bring all your batteries to bear at once. I expect Lord
Arlingford at any moment.

"Faithfully yours,
"CINCINNATUS Q. BRIGGS."

He put this letter into an envelope, and, addressing it to Dick
Saville at Claridge's, touched a bell.

"See that this goes at once," said he to the servant who appeared at
the sound of the bell and took the letter. This done, the American
turned once more to his papers.

"Let me see," soliloquized he : "where is that girl's letter? Ah!
here it is. *My dear cousin,— You are very kind, but I am quite old
enough to take care of myself.*—Yes, quite old enough, but, unfortunately, neither ugly nor poor enough.—*If I had wanted you to take
care of me, I should have married you years ago.*—How devilish cruel a
woman can be when she thinks fit!—*I don't like to say hard things of
a woman, but I am sorry to say I cannot sympathize with the lady who
was Lord Arlingford's wife,*—you surprise me, my dear cousin!—*and
I must take his word before hers,*—naturally, poor little girl! Um—m.
That young woman means business: we Briggs's generally do. It's
lucky for her I came to Europe when I did; otherwise she'd have flung
herself away on this fellow to a certainty. But I think, my lord Arlingford, that you have reached the end of your rope, and I'll lay odds
that it isn't from any scruple of your own that it doesn't hang you.
Well, I came to Europe for excitement, and, egad! I'm likely to get a
genteel sufficiency of it to-night. Thanks to you, my lord, I witnessed
the beginning, and am about to witness the end, of one of the liveliest
sensations that London has known for a good many years."

At this point Mr. Briggs's soliloquy was interrupted by the entrance of a servant announcing Dick Saville.

"Mr. Saville!" exclaimed Briggs, "delighted to see you. You're early; but you can't have got my letter yet?"

"Letter?" replied Dick: "what letter? No. I only dropped in on my way to fetch my wife, to ask how things were going on. I dined at the Club to try and find out if anything fresh had happened. I've brought the papers for Arlingford to sign: here they are in duplicate."

Mr. Briggs took them and glanced over one.

"I think Captain Goddard must be a remarkably forgiving man, to consider such a reparation sufficient," observed he. "On my side of the water a man in his position would, I fear, fill a man in Arlingford's with leaden bullets, and the jury would differ singularly on the verdict to be returned."

"I said something of the sort to him," returned Saville. "But he pointed out to me that there was nothing to be gained, but rather the reverse, from greater publicity. All he insists upon is that Arlingford should sign this Statutory Declaration and leave the country at once."

"Do you think that he will do it?"

"I think he will; but one can never be sure of such a blackguard. I shouldn't be very much surprised if at the last moment he didn't turn up."

"He told me he would be here at nine o'clock, but I confess I shouldn't be astonished if he weakened at the last moment. I must say, he has reduced the art of bluff to an applied science. When I advised him to give up my cousin, telling him we had the means to compel him to do so, his defiance was superb. I hope for all our sakes that the Baroness Altdorff possesses the power she promises to use with such effect. I tell you, dealing with him is no child's play! No, *sir!*"

"Well, I congratulate you on being quit of him as far as your cousin is concerned."

"How? quit of him?"

"Yes," replied Saville: "owing to very singular circumstances, he will make no further attempt to marry her."

"Is that really so? And these circumstances are——?"

"Eight thousand a year! Did you ever remark, Mr. Briggs, that the greatest scoundrels always get the best kind of love, and that a certain kind of good woman will cling to the man she has chosen—in the face of every reason why she should *not*—with a strength that she would display in no other cause? Well, such a woman is Lady Arlingford. She insists on going back to him."

"No!"

"It is so nevertheless. She has come into eight thousand a year, and proposes to invest it in Arlingford and connubial respectability. This relieves you of all personal anxiety. Lady Arlingford is ready to leave England with him. It only remains for us to see that he signs this document."

"And when will the Baroness—Bella-Demonia—arrive?"

"In good time. She is a capricious mystery, that woman, but her power is enormous. She demands that we unquestioningly submit to her instructions to-night. She refuses to tell us what power she holds over Arlingford, and exacts a meeting with Lady Arlingford before her identity is made known. Altogether, the evening promises to be eventful. By Jove! it's time I ran round for my wife. *Au revoir!* I'll be back inside a quarter of an hour."

And Dick Saville left the room. As he did so, the servant entered with a card, which Briggs read, an expression of perplexity crossing his face.

"Carteret?" he said,—"Major Homer Carteret? The name seems somehow familiar, but I can't place the man."

"The gentleman said he would be much obliged if you could see him for one moment," said the servant.

"Well, for one moment—show him up."

Major Carteret swung into the room on his best stride.

"I must apologize for calling at this unseemly hour," said he. "You don't remember me, Mr. Briggs. We met at Lord Arlingford's—er—some time ago."

"No apology is necessary," replied Mr. Briggs, gravely. "I remember perfectly. Pray be seated. Er—you wished to see me?"

"It is by Lord Arlingford's request that I am here. I came to say that he cannot be here so soon as he anticipated. Most important business——"

"So I expected," interrupted Briggs. "I think it very judicious——"

"Pardon me, Mr. Briggs," interrupted the major, in turn, "you are mistaken. The business that detains Lord Arlingford is as unexpected as it is urgent,—so urgent that he was unable to keep his appointment with me at the Club: he sent me a line asking me particularly to come here at once, fearing that you might misconstrue his absence. Erghem! I am very glad to have this opportunity of talking over this unhappy affair. I saw Lady Arlingford yesterday afternoon, and after we had discussed the matter she decided to make Arlingford an offer which I shall advise him to accept."

"May I ask if the offer concerns me in any way?" observed Mr. Briggs.

"Most certainly. Her ladyship's offer will cause Lord Arlingford to resign Miss Briggs's hand. Erghem! I have always had a great regard for Lady Arlingford, and it is her wish to re-marry her ex-husband."

"I have heard something of this a few moments ago."

"She looks upon it as the right thing to do for the child's sake, and, though I don't profess to be better than my neighbor, I must say that I agree with her."

And the major inflated his chest till he looked like a police-sergeant.

"I believe," said Mr. Briggs, drily, "that the amount of Lady Arlingford's income through the recent death of her aunt is now eight thousand a year. Am I not accurate, Major Carteret?"

"Quite; but——"

"As Lord Arlingford's *friend*," pursued the American, in the same tone, "you understand, of course, that on the interview of to-night depend his personal liberty, and, consequently, his *ability* to accept his late wife's offer."

"His liberty?"

"He will have to make full confession of his share in the conspiracy by which Captain Goddard was ruined. Er—please be seated. We shall spare Lady Arlingford as much as possible, but Captain Goddard's vindication is the first consideration. Frankly, if he refuses we shall convict him—and his accomplices—of conspiracy and criminal libel. Er—*please* be seated. I have been drawn into this matter by my cousin's unfortunate infatuation for Lord Arlingford."

"Mr. Briggs," replied the major, "I—I feel it is only due to myself to say that though I am, as you observe, Lord Arlingford's friend, I am deeply grieved at the part he took in that unfortunate business."

"I expected as much, and I am sure you are. Your good feeling in the matter simplifies a request I am about to make. Er—we are perfectly prepared to do without your testimony against him, but it might hasten matters to have it. How much do you want for it?"

Mr. Briggs leaned back complacently as Major Carteret sprang to his feet.

"Sir!" shouted he, "how dare you? I—er—er—— Five hundred pounds."

"*Please* be seated."

The major sat down.

"You shall have that amount to-night after the meeting. For the present, good-evening. You will be back in half an hour, if you please."

"Certainly," replied the warrior, and, taking his hat, he took with it his departure.

Mr. Briggs looked after him for a moment, his head slightly on one side.

Then he carefully selected a cigarette, which he thoughtfully lit. Then, walking to the fireplace to deposit the match, he slowly winked at himself in the pier-glass.

CHAPTER V.

REAPING THE WHIRLWIND.

MR. CINCINNATUS Q. BRIGGS's complacent appreciation of his own diplomacy was interrupted by the sudden irruption of Kitty Saville, followed by Dick.

"How d'ye do, Mr. Briggs?" was her greeting. "Dick wanted me not to come. The idea!—as if I would miss seeing my old friend Aubyn Goddard set right. What a long time it is since we met, and how queer that we should both be mixed up in this dreadful business! I little thought, when I sat next to you at dinner and was so impertinent to you, that night at Lord Arlingford's, that the evening would end so tragically. I suppose you heard about Lady Arlingford's long illness?"

"Yes, but not the whole of the trouble," replied Briggs, surprised at finding himself getting in a word edgeways.

"Well, you know, when she recovered she did nothing but blame herself for the whole affair. I believe that if Lord Arlingford had not been so careless of all decency, she would have begged his pardon. Her people insisted on a divorce, though, and she was too weak to oppose it, and when she got well she confided to me that if ever she found an opportunity she meant to ask him to marry her over again."

"But why?"

"For the sake of her child. Oh, what silly women these good women are! I'm so glad I'm a bad one! I was so impatient with her that we nearly quarrelled; and now that Dick has determined that Goddard shall be set right, she has begged to be allowed to come and give Arlingford one more chance. Oh, that woman is too much of an angel——"

"My *dear* Kitty," mildly expostulated Dick, "will you confine your attention to the matter in hand, and not expand on your personal feelings?"

"My *dear* Dick," was the reply, "will you let me say one word without interruption? Mr. Briggs is an old friend of mine: we met but once, it is true, but it's all the same; we should have been old friends if we had met more frequently: shouldn't we, Mr. Briggs?"

"My *dear* madam," answered the American, "you overwhelm me. To have met you but once, is both a privilege and a privation. It is to have lived and to have ceased living at the same moment. It is——"

"Mr. Briggs! if you finish that sentence I shall have a fit! I'm not accustomed to it. Dick when he intends to be most polite generally says, 'I say, old gal, you're not looking half bad to-night,' or when he means to be most affectionate, 'Here, Tramp! come and be smacked.'"

"Really, my dear," broke in Dick at this point, "these domestic details,—really——" And, at a loss for words to balance his wife's eloquence, he raised her hand deferentially to his lips.

"Why, Dick," exclaimed she, looking at him in alarm, "you're not well. All this excitement has been too much for you. Sit down, and don't talk. Oh, Mr. Briggs, I had a most mysterious little note from Lady Arlingford, just as I was starting to come here. Let me see: what did I do with it? Ah, here it is."

She took a letter from her pocket and read as follows:

"*I have heard terrible news this afternoon, and am nearly mad with hope and fear. I will explain all to you. I must speak to the lady whom you call Bella-Demonia alone: so when we meet to-night make some excuse to leave us together for a few minutes. Read this to Mr. Briggs, and ask him to manage with you to do as I wish.*—What does it mean?"

She laid the letter down on the writing-table. As she did so, she uttered a little exclamation, and, turning to Briggs, quoth very gravely,—

"Oh! I am so much obliged."

"I am charmed, of course; but *why?*" returned Briggs, in amazement.

"Because at last you've satisfied me that you *are* an American. Now, I wonder if you got this purposely for me, or if it's a toy?"

Her glance had fallen on the little revolver, and, taking it up, she brandished it with glee.

"Be careful, for gracious' sake!" exclaimed Briggs, in alarm. "It's loaded; and, though it's very small, it would kill at this range."

"Oh, goodness!" cried Kitty, as she dropped the weapon among the papers in comic consternation. "But come, what do you make of Lady Arlingford's note?"

"I can make nothing of it. At all events, her request is simple enough. They will both be here in a few moments, and if you will come into the library I should like to show you some etchings I have bought,—a Seymour-Haden, a couple of Wilfrid Ball's, and a Haig or two. I am told they're very fine."

"I should like to see them very much," returned Kitty, "though I don't understand them a bit."

Mr. Cincinnatus Q. Briggs was a most disappointing American. Instead of buying diamonds or pictures to sell, he spent his spare cash on rare bric-à-brac, etchings, and engravings to keep. You might be with him for twenty-four hours and never hear what anything he possessed had cost him. He had not the vaguest conception as to the price of his wines, and, though as ardent a collector of early-printed books and first editions as the most uneducated Westerner settled in New York, he positively knew what books he had, and had "read at" all of them. It is probable that had he been a married man the house he lived in would not have been made over to his wife to cheat his creditors in the event of financial shipwreck.

Kitty was still pondering when Lady Arlingford was announced. Briggs advanced to conduct her to a chair.

"I hope you are not fatigued, Lady Arlingford," said he. "Have you seen Captain Goddard yet?"

"Not yet," replied she. "I expected to find him here. Ah, Kitty, how happy you look! I'm so glad, dear! You got my letter?"

"Yes, dear, but I don't understand it. Have you seen the Baroness Altdorff?"

"Yes,—this afternoon, by accident; and I learnt from her the truth."

"The truth?"

"Yes. She told me who she was and is."

"Who is she? what is she?" exclaimed Dick and Kitty both together.

"You do not know?"

"No. Who is she?"

"*The Princess Galitzin.*"

The words were uttered by a servant who at this moment threw open the folding doors and admitted Bella-Demonia to the presence of three people whose faces took on an expression of unspeakable amazement.

"Oh, Dick," whispered Kitty, "who *is* she going to turn out to be next? Are you sure—are you *sure* that she is not Mrs. Richard Saville, among other things?"

"I swear she isn't," replied the no less astonished Dick, in the same tone.

"She'll be somebody else in a minute. I know she will."

"Probably."

Meanwhile, Mr. Briggs, leading the new-comer forward, said to Lady Arlingford,—

"Lady Arlingford, allow me to present to you——"

"The princess and I have already met," said her ladyship.

"Yes," returned Bella-Demonia, "and Mrs. and Mr. Saville I already know. How are you?"

"I was just going—as we have a few minutes yet—to show Mrs. Saville some pet etchings of mine," said Mr. Briggs. "Would you care to see them, princess?"

The Princess Galitzin exchanged a glance with Lady Arlingford, and then answered,—

"Thank you; I would rather see them later, if you will allow me, but do not let me deprive Mr. and Mrs. Saville of the pleasure. I do not feel quite up to enjoying etchings just now."

"Nor I," said Lady Arlingford.

"Well, then," pursued Mr. Briggs, "if you will pardon us for a while——?"

"By all means."

As Kitty left the room, she whispered to Lady Arlingford,—

"Are you sure you are strong enough? Shall I stay?"

"No, no: leave us," was the reply, and the next moment the two women were once more alone.

Lady Arlingford rose. "Will you give me your hand?" she said. "After hearing your story, I don't feel fit to touch you. I must have provoked you beyond endurance by my ignorance. Can you find it in your heart to forgive me?"

"If I could wipe out your injuries as easily as I can forgive you,— if indeed there is anything to forgive,—I do so a thousand times over. Can you believe that in knowing your trouble I have forgotten my own? How I wish I could help you! how I should like to prove the depth and reality of my sympathy!"

"You can prove it, and, if you will, you can give me all the peace I can hope to gain out of this sad life. If I should ask something of you that will tax your goodness to its depths, would you grant me my prayer? God knows I feel I have no right to expect so much from you; but——"

"There is no effort I would spare to help you. What can I do?"

"I implore you to give Jack—Lord Arlingford—one chance to clear himself of some of the charges of which you think him guilty. That horrible story you told me—there must be some explanation. Let him speak in his own behalf. I *know* he will do his utmost to repair the injury he did Aubyn, and I am sure Aubyn will bury the past, if only for my sake. Will you not do the same? Influential, protected as you are in your own country, surely you have only to ask for the annulment of your marriage with my—my—husband, to obtain it. Is it not so?"

"Yes; but why do you ask?"

"Because I would help him to atone for his past; because if you will give him his freedom I will still take him back. Oh, don't shrink from me! Hear what I have to say before you condemn me. Remember, I have a child. It is my duty to do all in my power to bring her father back to her."

"And you would live with that man, despising him as you must, because you feel it to be your duty?"

"Even so! It is the least I can do to atone to my little girl for the wrong that has been done her. I should be unable to meet her eyes, as she asks for her father, if I had not done all in my power to redeem him. Will you do what I ask?"

The Princess Galitzin rose, and, walking to the window, appeared to reflect deeply. Then she came back, and said,—

"For your sake, I promise that so far as my own injuries are concerned I will forgive him. But his ruin of Aubyn Goddard I cannot —will not forgive. Not upon me, but on his confession to-night, will depend his liberty. His fate is in his own hands."

"Ah! how can I thank you? I am confident now."

At this moment Mr. Briggs entered the room.

"Captain Goddard has just arrived," said he. "Shall I bring him in here?"

"One moment," said Lady Arlingford. "I—I can bear no more to-night. May I ask you, Mr. Briggs, to let me rest awhile in another room, and then I will go home."

"Certainly: it shall be as you wish," replied Mr. Briggs. "Come in here. I will see that your carriage is ready at any moment."

Her ladyship turned to the princess and extended her hand as she said,—

"May I see you once more before I leave England? I don't know if I am doing what is right, but I hope so."

Bella-Demonia bent her head, and Lady Arlingford left the room with Mr. Briggs.

Left alone, the woman looked after the departing form, and said, half aloud,—

"Who shall say that you are wrong? Not I, indeed,—I who have forgotten my revenge in my new-born dream." She pressed her hands to her head, and turned, just as Aubyn Goddard entered the room.

They faced each other for a few moments without speaking, and then Goddard, advancing, took both her hands in his.

"So I am to thank you for honor as well as for life," said he, gravely.

"That sounds almost like a reproach," replied she. "Have I not done everything I could to atone for my share in the disaster I so unwittingly brought on you? Besides, it was your delirium, and not the prince, that detained you at Deve-kiui. As far as he was concerned, you were free to go as you had come."

"He is a wonderful man. Having caught me, I wonder he did not kill me: I had given him trouble enough. Besides, he would have been killing two birds with one stone,—or rather two men with one bullet. That evening when I lay unconscious at your feet—yours and his—the scene must have been terrible: it is never out of my mind."

"It is one of the few moments of my life that I am ashamed of. When the prince recognized you and I knew my trick to save you had been useless, I gave up all hope, and in the desperation of the moment I offered to buy your life from him. 'Only let him escape,' said I, 'and I promise never to see him again, and I—my life—shall be given to you!'"

"My God! And what did he say?"

"He said, simply, 'I have loved you as long as I have known you, and you evidently do not understand that emotion as I do. I hope to show you that I can be at the same time a disappointed lover and—a gentleman.' That was all that was said till you were on the high-road to recovery and we laid our plans for the trapping of Arlingford. I am not ashamed to say that I fell on my knees and asked his pardon. It was he who planned and devised so that your capture and whereabouts should be kept a secret from Skobeleff."

"How generous!"

"It was well for you that your wound proved so dangerous, and that before you could be moved peace was proclaimed at San Stefano."

Aubyn Goddard raised her hand to his lips, and said, in a voice that betrayed the depth of his emotion,—

"And you have borne all this for me! I wonder why?"

"Why?" answered Bella-Demonia, with a quick smile and shake of her head. "Because you are personally very distasteful to me; because, in short, I do not like you; because we are antipathetic to each other; because you have been so nobly treated that you deserve no sympathy. Are these reasons enough, Aubyn?"

And the man, who was just a man and no longer Aubyn Goddard the Hero, clasped to his breast the woman, who was just a woman and no longer Bella-Demonia the Mystery, as she lay in his arms and gave up her soul to the ecstasy of his kiss.

They were very nearly caught by Mr. Briggs, who entered the room at the moment, or rather just after it.

"Princess," said he, "Lord Arlingford is here. Shall he come in?"

"Wait one moment," returned she. "My plan is much upset by Lady Arlingford's strange determination, but I have promised her my aid. If he signs the papers I am willing to avoid seeing him, and it will be best that he should not know that I have found him. Let me retire for a while, where I can hear what he has to say. This conservatory will do."

"It shall be as you wish," answered Mr. Briggs, showing her to a little conservatory built out over the porch of the house, communicating by a French window with the apartment. As she turned towards it she gave her hand to Goddard, who bent and kissed it.

" Oh !" observed Mr. Briggs to himself. " Ah !"

Then he went to the door and admitted Dick Saville, accompanied by Arlingford and Major Carteret. The gallant major was evidently very nervous : he stood a little apart from his principal and twisted his moustache spasmodically, a fit subject for an artist who might desire to make a " Study of a Man, ratting."

Mr. Briggs motioned the four men to be seated, and took his place at the writing-table. Then, slightly clearing his throat, he observed,—

" As we all know for what purpose we are here, it will, I think, only be necessary for me to read this statutory declaration, which has been drawn up in duplicate for the signature of his lordship."

Arlingford signified his attention, and Mr. Briggs continued :

" The declaration reads as follows : ' I, John Vyvian Fane, Viscount Arlingford, do hereby solemnly declare that the charges made by me against Captain the Honorable Aubyn Goddard were false ; that I made the said charges knowing them to be false, and with a specific purpose which was accomplished in the failure of his mission.' Now, Lord Arlingford, if you will affix your signature in the presence of witnesses, we can terminate this very painful meeting."

Arlingford sprang to his feet.

" Sign that !" he cried. " I refuse to sign it ! I am willing to say that to the best of my belief I made a mistake ; but sign such a monstrous production as that ? Certainly not !"

" You know the alternative, Lord Arlingford," said Dick Saville.

" I have told you what I will do," retorted Arlingford, turning upon him, " and there is no power on earth that can force me to do more."

" Perhaps *I* can persuade Lord Arlingford to sign," said a quiet, rich voice behind them, as Bella-Demonia stepped into the room. Hearing the words, Arlingford started violently and turned to meet the woman's stare.

" Carita Galitzin !" he exclaimed. " My God !"

" Hardly that," replied the princess, in mock deprecation, " but, unfortunately, your wife."

" His wife !" The exclamation broke forth simultaneously from the other four. Goddard started as if he had been shot, and went quickly to the woman's side.

" What do you mean ?" he said, in a husky undertone.

" Wait," she replied.

Meanwhile, Arlingford, with a violent effort, had recovered his self-control.

" You will have," said he, sneeringly, " some difficulty in proving that the very hurried form that we went through was a legal marriage, even in Russia, and you will doubtless be too sensible to risk proving yourself to have been my mistress."

Goddard, with a half-cough of rage, sprang at him, but was restrained by Saville and by the princess, who stepped between them.

" Unfortunately," said she, in a tone of withering scorn, " to have been your wife is, if possible, the greater disgrace. You overestimate the honor of a marriage with yourself, and you underestimate the fact that you are in no position to oppose my slightest whim."

" Indeed ?　Because——?"

" Because on me depends not only your ability to obtain the means of subsistence, but your liberty, your very life itself, belong to me.　I have but to hold up my finger and your doom is sealed.　You will sign that document *at once.*"

" Charming !" returned Arlingford ; " but we are in England now, and I am prepared to defend any action you may choose to bring.　I refuse to sign.　Do your worst!　I defy you !" he concluded, violently.

" Mr. Briggs," said the princess, " I saw Prince Schouloff's carriage below.　Will you be so good as to call him ?　Thanks."

And Mr. Cincinnatus Q. Briggs left the room.

" In all the years," resumed the princess, coming close to Arlingford, " during which I sought for the murderer of my brother, I thought that nothing but his death could appease me.　Now, however, fortunately for you, I have found a man whose honor is as pure as God's blessed mercy, a man by comparison with whom you are too unclean a thing even to kill."

She turned on her heel and returned to Goddard's side as Mr. Briggs re-entered the room, accompanied by Prince Schouloff.

" Prince," said Carita Galitzin to the Chief of Police, " will you kindly tell Lord Arlingford that if necessary we shall not be wanting in proofs to substantiate our charges of bigamy, nor shall we shrink from the publicity consequent on taking steps to frustrate his present plans ?"

" The prince will doubtless remember," said Arlingford, with a cool assurance that was sublime, " that the onus of disproof lies with the accused, and that I am in my own country and therefore have the best chance of assuming the character of accuser.　You, as foreigners, will have to go through certain formalities before being able to institute legal proceedings.　I shall therefore proceed at once to prove that yours is simply an attempt at blackmail."

" I am compelled to admit that Lord Arlingford's view of the legal position is entirely correct," replied Prince Schouloff, quietly.

Had a thunder-bolt fallen among them, the consternation of his auditors could not have been more lively.

" You agree with him !" exclaimed the princess.

" I am so sure of his accuracy," returned the prince, calmly, " that I have taken the very position he so clearly points out to be the best.　The negotiations pending between our respective governments have enabled me to procure a warrant for the immediate arrest of John Vyvian Fane, Viscount Arlingford, and it will be in Petersburg—not in London—that his lordship will have to answer the charge."

" What charge ?"

" Murder."

" Murder !" echoed Arlingford, his air of cynic assurance suddenly changing to one of alarmed concern.　" You can scarcely charge a man with that of which he is ignorant.　You can *charge* him with whatever you please, but I learn for the first time that I have killed any one.　Preposterous !　May I know whom I murdered ?"

" You will find all duly stated in this warrant," answered the prince, handing him a paper. "Your long residence in Russia, and, above all, your connection with the police, render you sufficiently conversant with our code to convince you that we are acting within our right, and," added he, significantly, "that we seldom act in vain."

"Your methods are at least expensive," ejaculated Arlingford.

"You are well able to judge of that point. My officers are below: you will, I presume, accompany them without further trouble.—Mr. Briggs, will you allow me to write some instructions? Thank you."

And the prince seated himself at the writing-table, whilst Arlingford stared dazedly at the warrant that he held in his hands. A servant appeared and handed a slip of paper to Mr. Briggs, who whispered to the princess. The latter left the room, as Dick Saville approached Prince Schouloff and remarked,—

"Prince, this is a desperate accusation,—and so unexpected."

"Desperate diseases," returned the prince, "require desperate remedies. I feared that he might be unmanageable: so I took this precaution."

"But shall you be able to prove him guilty?"

"That is quite unimportant," was the answer. "Lord Arlingford will doubtless be glad to sign any document before his trial, rather than return to Russia. You understand?"

"May I ask," said Mr. Briggs, who had joined them, "when and where this murder was committed?"

"God knows: I don't," returned the prince, laconically, as he turned once more to his writing.

Mr. Briggs's free and enlightened American mind was confused.

"But surely——" he began.

"My dear fellow," said Dick Saville, taking him aside, "what the deuce is the use of being a Russian prince if you can't prove a man guilty of anything you like on an emergency?"

Meanwhile, Aubyn Goddard had approached the diplomat.

"I am much indebted to you——" he began.

"Not at all," interrupted Schouloff. "I was unfortunate enough to be a party—for reasons of state—to your trouble; it is but right that I should be a party to your vindication. I repeat, for reasons of state I was compelled to act as I did, knowing that I could vindicate you at the right moment. That act was as repugnant to me in the manner of its performance, as to give you my assistance to-day is a pleasure."

Lord Arlingford had finished the perusal of the warrant, and had scribbled a few words in his note-book which he gave to Major Carteret for delivery to his wife. Now he moved towards the door. There he turned and faced the five men. The Princess Galitzin and Mrs. Bradley Dashton entered the room behind and unobserved by him.

"You calculated with perfect certainty," said his lordship, with a brave show of defiance, "and I am not fool enough to resist you and give you the chance of killing me ' in self-defence.' Fortunately, my wife is in a position to institute proceedings, which will be done at once. Egad! you're all very clever, but I observe that Captain Goddard's little card-trick remains still unexplained. The disappearance of that king of trumps *was* queer, wasn't it? Let me see: I think the suit was clubs."

"You need not tax your memory," said a voice—"Bella-Demonia's" —behind him. "The card is here!" She laid it on the table, and all bent forward to look at it. "You see," pursued the princess, "that this card is one bearing on its back the monogram of a gambling-club to which Lord Arlingford belonged, which was immediately afterwards broken up. The other,—the one held by Captain Goddard,—a two of clubs, will be forthcoming if required. *This* card was given to Mrs. Dashton to destroy, that night, by Lord Arlingford. Fortunately, she did not do so. The reason of Captain Goddard's refusal to show that two of clubs has been explained: so that the signing of this declaration is no longer necessary."

"You will state fully," said Dick Saville to Mrs. Dashton, who was leaning against the writing-table, "how and when this card came into your possession?"

"In any terms you choose to dictate," she said.

Arlingford had been staggered for the moment, but came up to time, game to the last.

"I congratulate you all," said he, with an evil sneer, "on the value of *Mrs. Dashton's* word!"

"You will find that it is to be depended on," said Mrs. Dashton, quietly. "I told you this afternoon that——"

"That I was to do a great many things," broke in Arlingford, in his former tone. "Among others, that I was to marry *you*."

"No; I told you that you should marry no other."

"And *I* told *you* that a man does not marry his——"

"Stop!" cried the woman, her eyes blazing with fury. Her glance fell on the revolver lying under her hand: quick as thought she raised it and fired. Lord Arlingford fell heavily to the ground, mortally wounded.

Amid the general consternation, the Princess Galitzin went to Mrs. Dashton's side. She was fainting.

"Whew! what shall we do now?" said Dick Saville to Prince Schouloff.

"Mrs. Dashton is one of my witnesses," returned he. "I will see that she leaves the country at once. She will never return."

A door was thrown open, and Lady Arlingford rushed into the room. Seeing her husband lying on the floor, she flung herself by his side.

"My God!" she cried, "how did this happen?"

Arlingford, with a supreme effort, raised himself, and, making a sign imposing silence on the others, addressed his wife:

"I—I—the game was up," he said. "I—I—shot myself. Poor little woman! you are well rid of me."

He sank into her arms.

John Vyvian Fane, Viscount Arlingford, was dead.

THE END.

www.ingramcontent.com/pod-product-compliance
Lightning Source LLC
Chambersburg PA
CBHW022341020726
47500CB00004B/1230